A S

Leo was recognised to be the most outstanding surgeon at the Central London
Hospital, but he was hardly a convention-
al romantic figure. So who would have
guessed that his affair with his frail young
secretary Judith—who was threatened by
a disabling illness—would turn out to be
the greatest love story the hospital had
ever known?

# A SURGEON'S LIFE

BY
ELIZABETH HARRISON

MILLS & BOON LIMITED
15–16 BROOK'S MEWS
LONDON W1A 1DR

*First published in Great Britain 1983
by Robert Hale Limited*

*This edition published 1984 by Mills & Boon Limited*
© Elizabeth Harrison 1983

*Australian copyright 1984
Philippine copyright 1984*

ISBN 0 263 74851 0

03–1084

*Photoset by Rowland Phototypesetting Ltd
Bury St Edmunds, Suffolk
Made and printed in Great Britain by
Richard Clay (The Chaucer Press) Ltd
Bungay, Suffolk*

# Chapter 1

The buildings that housed the Central London Hospital were more of an architect's nightmare than a dream of the future, its staff were apt to remark sarcastically. The original medieval *hôtel-Dieu* was hidden away in an inner cobbled yard, as beautiful now as it had been in the twelfth century, and fronted by a Georgian sash-windowed house of pink brick, recently cleaned, its lines still wonderfully satisfying to the eye. But there it ended. Two Victorian Gothic wings, highly ornamented and pretentious, had been the subject of derision and unkind comment for years, though – surrounded as they were now by the twentieth century's bleak contributions – they were at last developing a charm of their own.

The futuristic modern tower built in the Seventies was the new surgical block. Here they started work early, and on this fine morning in April a preoccupied crowd – physicians, surgeons, anaesthetists, nurses, technicians, porters – was converging on it.

A beautiful West Indian girl in a scarlet-lined cloak over a sister's dark blue went through the wide, sliding glass doors, and shortly afterwards an oddly blank-faced man in a dark suit was decanted from a Volvo driven by a tawny-haired girl, while a burly surgeon came strolling round the corner, frowning and thoughtful, but unhurried. Leo Rosenstein.

Up in the general surgery theatre they were edgy,

and Stella Jarvis, whose first day it was as sister, most jittery of all. She told herself not to be ridiculous. She could handle whatever came up. And Leo Rosenstein was recognised to be one of the most capable and organised surgeons in the hospital. She was looking forward to working for him, and determined not only to make a success of her new post but to enjoy it. Latterly, enjoyment of any sort had been conspicuous by its absence from her days – and even more from her nights. For Stella was broken-hearted. Tall, slight and delicately coffee-coloured with silky black hair and wonderful brown eyes, she was agreed on all sides to be among the loveliest of the Central's sisters – who were not, as a group, short on looks. But her love-life at present was non-existent. That this was her own responsibility failed to raise her morale from the depths to which it had slumped after her separation from Laurence Bridge, the registrar in neurosurgery with whom she'd been living since she'd been a second-year student, and certainly did nothing to fill the aching void his departure had left.

Her new chief might do that. She hoped so, anyway. She knew, of course, that he could put his juniors through it. He demanded high standards from his entire team – intermittent flashes of brilliant inspiration were not enough. Leo demanded the sort of genius that included an infinite capacity for taking pains. Meticulous himself, he expected a thorough grasp of detail from everyone round him, and gave them hell on wheels if they failed in any way, she'd been told. But, they also said, he was fundamentally kind, and seldom hit hard where it could really hurt. In any case, they'd reminded her, most surgeons went ape at least once during a list. The theatre took it for granted. She'd been warned, though, that since he didn't possess the six pairs of hands he could have done with, he did tend to behave as if the hands of anyone in his team would react as instantaneously to his every thought as if they were positioned on the extremities of his own arms. His assistants struggled to anticipate his every wish, reading his mind – they hoped – before he knew it himself. If they were not as fast as this, he'd swear at them. They were resigned to that.

Recently, though, they said, he'd become much more irritable, and had even begun throwing his instruments about on occasion, a habit he'd always condemned. Surgeons should not imagine they were in business as prima donnas, he'd announced often enough.

Since this was the Central London Hospital, where gossip was the breath of life, there had been a good deal of talk about this change in him, and a number of theories to account for it. In the surgeons' changing-room they were airing some of them. Leo's latest actress was going to New York, to open in that play. He was angry with her for leaving him, for putting her career first – before him. All this made him not only irascible but frustrated, too. Naturally.

'Leo? Frustrated?' Nick Waring, tall as his chief, but, unlike him, thin and serious-looking, was senior registrar in general surgery. 'That's a way-out diagnosis. He doesn't know the meaning of the word. Or the condition, either. Leo frustrated? That'll be the day.'

'If you ask me, it's nothing to do with the actress. It's Sister Henderson.' Jeremy Hillyard, Leo's registrar, was square and stocky and looked comfortably self-assured, though in reality he was one of the world's worriers. 'I reckon that when he grasped that she really meant to pack in working with him in this theatre it blew his mind. He had a flaming row with her about it, and now he doesn't know how to live with himself – or without her. He's freaked right out.' Jeremy had maintained for months that Leo's actresses were for fun and games, but that when he decided to settle down he'd make a good solid marriage with his theatre sister. Now suddenly she'd abandoned her station at his side and accepted a senior post – for which, admittedly, she was long overdue. This was the blow that had rocked him.

'Rubbish.' Nick was closer to Leo than most of them in the room. He'd been his house surgeon, his registrar, and now his senior registrar, while his wife Sophie was Leo's secretary. 'Who found him his new theatre sister? Sister Henderson herself. And the two of them had supper together only last night. I left them at it. He was dishing out veal in mushroom sauce from a vast casserole while she checked the timing of this morning's list – because of this extra case he's slipping in. Poor old Miss Kilpatrick.'

'Yes, he mentioned he was taking her first.' Jeremy forgot about gossip and girlfriends, and his chief's marital future held no more interest for him. He was unhappy about Miss Kilpatrick. 'Is she up to surgery, do you think?' he asked Nick.

'Probably not. And if anything's bugging Leo, it's that. Thinks we may lose her while she's on the table. He didn't want to do her. Only decided last night.'

'I'm surprised he's opening her up again, though. We all know she's inoperable. And very frail. So why go in again?'

'He says she's getting a lot of pain. He thinks if he opens her up again and relieves the pressure that's causing it, although it can only lead to a brief respite, it may be long enough for her to end her days in more comfort.'

'Not going to improve his results, if she dies on the table, is it?'

Nick, masked and gowned now, shot him a withering look. 'You're not going to suggest Leo would ever put his statistics before a patient in pain?'

'Both of us know plenty who would,' Jeremy retorted, unrepentant.

At that moment their chief himself came in, looking as glum as they'd feared. A big, bulky man, corpulent and powerful, with a large voice to match. 'Mornin'.' He was curt.

Nick's eyes met Jeremy's. Exactly as they'd forecast. Usually he was jovial when scrubbing up – too jovial for some of them so soon after breakfast. But today he was silent, washing and rinsing his arms methodically and staring morosely at the wall. He was thinking about Miss Kilpatrick. As Nick had surmised, he wasn't expecting her to come through. And he didn't want to lose her. He never liked losing a patient – who did? – but he was particularly sad at the thought of losing her. She was such a gallant indomitable old soul.

All right, so she was in her seventies, had had a good span of days. They'd been good years, too, he knew, from what she'd told him. She herself, of course, was ready to go. Prepared. She'd said as much. But he was going to hate losing her, and he'd had to struggle with himself before he could face the likelihood that he, by his surgical intervention, would very likely be the agent of her death. Today. This morning. On the table in his theatre.

It had been only three days ago that she'd come to see him in Harley Street. He'd examined her, listened to her, and questioned her – not that he needed to ask her much. She was a shadow of herself. She'd lost more weight since he'd last seen her, and she was a nasty muddy colour. She'd been unable to keep her food down, she said. She thought at first this was some temporary upset, but it had continued.

'We'll have you in, do some more tests and have some more X-rays,' he'd said.

'All right.' She agreed briskly. She'd been headmistress of a famous girl's school, and she might have been in her study. 'How long do you think I've got?'

He sighed, and his lower lip jutted out in the way his staff all recognised, when he didn't like what he found. 'May be a year,' he said. 'May be six months. Or it could be less. Three months.' They'd long ago established the habit of honesty, and he made no attempt to hide the truth from her. He patted her narrow shoulder. 'I can make you a good deal more comfortable than you are now, though,' he said. 'You should have come to see me sooner. You don't have to put up with this.'

She shrugged the bony shoulders. 'Wanted to keep going as long as I could,' she told him, still in the same brisk tone. 'Now, you're not to worry over me. If you can operate, so that I can have a square meal again and keep it down, I'll be very thankful. Even if it is a bit of a risk.'

A bit of a risk. One hell of a risk.

'The problem is – '

'I know what the problem is. You think I may not come through. But that doesn't matter. Frankly, if they give me my – what do you call it? My pre-medication, is that right? And then trundle me along to the theatre, and that's the last I know, I shan't be sorry. I've had a good life, but now it's come to this, and I've had about enough. You've looked after me wonderfully. I'm grateful to you, and if this turns out to be the end of the road, then so be it. You mustn't be upset. You won't be, will you?' She was pulling on her gloves – she had old-fashioned ways – and she suddenly darted a piercing look across the desk at him. 'You're far too soft-hearted, you know,' she told him. 'It must make problems for you. But I'm someone you can be easy in your mind about. So don't forget.' She rose to her feet. 'And thank you for everything.'

He walked round the desk, and took her arm. 'I'll see you out to the car.'

Outside the front door a bright little yellow Mini, driven by a middle-aged tweedy lady, pulled up as they appeared. This was routine. Miss Kilpatrick apparently had a rota of former pupils who ran a personal car service for her, all of them so competent – presumably they wouldn't make the rota otherwise – they could drive round the block for half an hour, yet appear at his door within seconds of Miss Kilpatrick's departure. Today he went down into the road with her and helped her into her seat. She adjusted her belt, and looked up brightly at him. 'I'll see you tomorrow, then.'

'That's right.'

'You're not to worry. I'm not going to, and you mustn't either. Promise me?'

'All right,' he said. 'I won't.'

She nodded, raised a gloved hand, and the car nipped smartly away into the traffic.

Leo trod heavily back up the steps. He'd promised her, and there was little he could do that he hadn't already done, so he wouldn't worry. But his spirits sagged. Miss Kilpatrick had put up tough resistance to the disease that had her in its grip. She'd battled strenuously for years, she'd never given in, but now at last it looked as though they were going to have to admit defeat. Over the years he'd grown very fond of her.

She'd had long periods in the private wing on her BUPA subscription – paid by the school – and he'd seen her three or four times a day for months at a time. They'd been oddly in sympathy, though an apparently unlikely pair, and they'd confided in one another more than once. Nothing very important. Odd little snippets about the past, about earlier hopes and fears or disappointments. But they'd become friends. Once or twice he'd been out to see her in her Hampstead flat – this had turned out to be one huge, high-ceilinged room with a great bay window overlooking the heath, with a tiny kitchenette and bathroom partitioned off it, in one of those great Edwardian mansions on the brow of the hill. She had given him tea out of eggshell china, and told him tales of her school, the room behind her packed with photographs and lovely old antique furniture she'd inherited. He'd reciprocated with a more or less unexpurgated version of various escapades from his student days at the Central, and she'd laughed so much her wasted old body had shaken the heavy armchair she occupied.

He shut off the tap's flow with his elbow, shook his hands so that the droplets spattered, dried them on the disposable towel he hated, and accepted the gloves held ready for him by one of the nurses.

She was his friend, and he was going to cut her open and in so doing very likely kill her. Almost certainly she wasn't up to this final intervention. He frowned, and met Nick's knowledgeable eyes. 'Come on,' Leo said gruffly. 'What are we all hanging about for, eh? Let's get on with it.'

He strode into the theatre, a large, gowned and, it seemed to his new theatre sister, angry man. Her heart sank.

'Mornin', Sister.' His voice was thick and discouraging.

Above the mask, two liquid brown eyes met his, and momentarily he was astonished that they were not Sister Henderson's familiar twinkling hazel.

'Good morning, Mr Rosenstein.' Sister Jarvis was formal. Inwardly she was panicking badly.

'Patient ready for me?' He glanced across to the anaesthetist.

'As ready as she'll ever be,' Robert Chasemore told him ominously. A consultant anaesthetist, the director of intensive care in general surgery, his mere presence at the patient's head was yet another indication of the risky nature of today's surgery. Stella Jarvis's heart sank even further towards her theatre clogs. It would have to happen to her. Her first case was going to die on the table.

'Right. We want to get this job done as fast as we can, you'll agree, Rob, in view of her poor condition.'

Robert Chasemore nodded. 'Quite so.'

'Better start, then, without more ado. Nothing to be gained by 'anging about. A midline incision, Nick, I think. That'll save us a fraction of time – and time is going to be precious. This patient, Sister, has been having pain and vomiting due, I'm sure, to pyloric stenosis. The purpose of this operation is simply to make 'er more comfortable by removing the obstruction which is causing the symptoms. That's all. No more. We'll have a quick look round, Nick, and then do a gastro-enterostomy. Off we go then.' He held an expectant gloved hand vaguely in Sister Jarvis's direction, and frowned. She put what she trusted to be the correct scalpel into it, and, since she was right, he made the first incision.

As he'd foreseen, the interior of Miss Kilpatrick's abdomen gave none of them any joy. Briefly the little group round the table under the searing light went still and silent. Leo, though, now that the worst was upon them, became almost cheerful. 'Yes, well,' he said, 'we knew it would be like this. But if I can deal with this little bit of trouble 'ere, she's goin' to feel a good deal better.'

Normally unhurried to the point of apparent lethargy – though slow was not a word any of them would have used to describe his technique – today he was so fast that even Nick, with all his years of working alongside him, could barely keep up. Sister Jarvis handed out instruments to both of them, prayed fervently for heavenly support in her ordeal, and wondered how long she'd been able to stand the pace.

'There now,' Leo said finally. 'We've been able to bypass the obstruction, and the stomach can empty pretty well through this new opening, I'd say. That's really quite nice, isn't it? In the circumstances. So now we'll get out.' He looked up, across to Robert Chasemore at the patient's head. 'How is she at your end, Rob?'

'I can still hold her steady. But the quicker you are the better.'

'We'll get out fast. Nick, we'll both sew up.' He gestured with his hand. 'That'll speed things up. Me from the top, you from the bottom. Thank you, Sister.'

When they'd finished, Miss Kilpatrick was still pink, still breathing.

'We seem to have made it.' Robert Chasemore failed to keep the astonishment out of his voice.

'So far so good.' Leo nodded. 'Over to you now.'

'I thought I'd stay on with her in intensive care for a while – my registrar will look after your next case.'

'The appendicectomy. Should be straightforward. Right. There we are, then.' He stood back from the table and straightened his massive shoulders. 'Thank you, everyone, Sister. Sorry you had such a tricky one for your first case – they won't all be like this, praise be. That certainly went a good deal better than we were anticipating, eh? Relief to us all.'

'There'd be time for a quick cup of coffee, Mr Rosenstein, if you'd like it.' Sister Jarvis thought he deserved one. 'Nurse tells me the next patient has only just arrived in the anaesthetic room. You've been so quick we're running ahead of schedule.'

'Thank you, Sister. I think we'll carry straight on, though, so they can bring the patient in as soon as they're ready.'

'Very good, sir.' Sister Jarvis signalled with her lovely brown eyes across the room to her staff nurse, who twitched an eyebrow back and departed for the anaesthetic room.

'I though we were in for a death on the table.' Nick spoke what everyone of them was feeling.

'So did I. Was dreading it, to be honest. Selfish of me, though. Patient wouldn't 'ave bin sorry, and it wouldn't 'ave done her no 'arm to've slipped away unknowing, as she told me herself only the other day. But there it is. I was feeling bad about it. Ruddy egoism rearing its ugly head again.'

'I don't think you should think that.' Nick was quick to dispute Leo's interpretation. 'It's more an occupational attitude of mind, it seems to me. If you spend twenty years learning to keep people alive, you can't be expected to welcome death with open arms.'

'Even when, perhaps, you should.' This was Jeremy, notorious for always questioning his own and everyone else's motives, usually to their disadvantage.

'So what would you've done about her, eh, Jeremy?' Leo was sharp. He might be ready to blame himself, but he wasn't standing back and accepting censure from his juniors.

'Me?' Jeremy frowned. 'I suppose,' he admitted uneasily, 'I'd have left her alone. I'd have been wrong, as this morning has proved.' It was a sort of an apology.

'And you, young Alec?' Leo, aggressive still, stared at his house surgeon, who in his opinion, as he'd put it to Nick the previous evening, was 'wet behind the lugholes, but thinks he's God's gift to medicine, going to be Moynihan and Alexander Fleming rolled into one, and all before he touches forty.'

'I'd have gone in. Like you, sir.' Alec was confident.

Leo sighed, and his eyes met Nick's. He hummed a little tune. 'When will they ever learn?' They all knew the words.

His house surgeon reddened, and Sister Jarvis smiled behind her mask. She thought she might be going to enjoy her new post, after all.

The anaesthetic registrar came in, as they wheeled the appendicectomy towards the table. The hour was approaching nine now, and the gallery was beginning to fill up with students.

By the time they reached the end of Leo's list it had emptied again, as its occupants felt the pangs of hunger and slipped away for a sandwich and coffee, though most of them were back in time for the final operation, even though it was no more than a routine inguinal hernia. Leo Rosenstein's operating sessions, like his ward rounds, were usually good value. His exposition was clear, his teaching the sort that went in and remained tucked away in a corner of the recipient's mind, ready to reappear on demand. He could, as a bonus, be hilariously funny. And then they loved his fruity London voice, so different from the pedantic bleat they heard around the more academic departments.

Leo now was at the height of his career. In his late thirties, he was a power in the hospital. He'd be, they were all sure of it, the next chairman of the medical committee.

And he'd come, as they were fond of reminding one another, from nowhere. Or, to be precise, from a well-known and very lowly position. From the fruit barrow outside the main entrance.

They were wrong. Hospital mythology, not for the first time, had muddled the details. It had been Leo's grandfather who had been a barrow boy. When Leo was born, the family already owned two green-groceries, one in Great St. Anne's near the hospital, the other in Gray's Inn Road, half a mile to the east. The grandparents lived over one shop, Leo's parents over the other. But when his father died – young, in his middle forties – he'd left Leo a chain of prosperous shops stretching out into the suburbs.

From the beginning, the Central had recognised that Leo Rosenstein was going to be outstanding. Indeed, with his Cockney voice straight from the slums and his boisterous, untutored ways, he needed to be. He'd refused to moderate his voice – there were some who said he deliberately exaggerated its uncouth vowels in order to shock and annoy, though as the years rolled by his utterances became a very personal blend of cockney rhythms and consultant's phraseology.

His voice apart, he'd changed along the road to the top. Alongside his slick surgery he had acquired immense skill, not only in clinical management, but, when the occasion demaded it, a poised control that took charge of any situation anywhere. No one at the Central would have been particularly surprised, these days, to see him suddenly surface in any odd corner of the globe, running things. He might be chairman of an oilrig or leader of the House of Lords. There was nothing they'd put past him. However, what he had in fact done, after two years as Resident Surgical Officer at the hospital – the top surgical post before a consultancy – was to go into his chief's firm. Five years ago, or more, that had been, and the news had stunned the hospital. Leo Rosenstein, of all people, on Lord Mummery's firm.

Mummery had retired now, and Leo had taken over his big consulting-room in Harley Street, though he retained his own flat in the nineteenth-century block near the hospital, putting Nick and Sophie Waring into the rooms on the top floor in Harley Street that had been Lord Mummery's city home for years. Here they lived, while Nick ran the department of general surgery and the slight, blonde, fragile-looking Sophie – who in fact was blazingly competent and tough as they come – continued to mastermind Leo's appointments, correspondence, lecture notes, case histories, travel arrangements and income tax.

After his list, he went along to Harley Street to sign his letters. Sophie, he found, had another girl with her – someone he was certain he ought to recognise. Tall and very slender, with hair like autumn leaves, wide-set grey eyes that reminded him at once of someone, though he couldn't think who, and a pale oval face that came close to real beauty. Who was she? He ought to know.

'You know Judith Chasemore, don't you?' Sophie read his blank expression unerringly, and rescued him.

'Sure I do,' he lied, his mind racing. Robert Chasemore's daughter, who'd been ill in some mysterious way that Rob refused to discuss. 'How are you getting on?' he enquired cautiously.

What was the latest information about the girl? Rob must surely have given him some clue – what had he said?

# Chapter 2

Judith Chasemore saw Leo's assessing glance flick across her, and experienced, not for the first time, a spurt of resentment. This was how they all looked at her these days. Diagnostically, as if she were a patient in the ward and had no other existence. A non-person. Part of their professional day, a suitable vehicle for the exercise of their skills.

Perhaps she could have become used to that. But accompanying it, inevitably, came their swift recollection that as well as a patient she was Robert Chasemore's daughter, and a physiotherapy student, too. Then the iron curtain came right down, their faces were immediately schooled to utter blankness as they concealed their thoughts from her – their doubts, their fears, their awareness of the uncertainty of her future. They knew exactly how to deal with patients, or alternatively, with friends and colleagues. But with the daughter of a colleague, who was also a patient, they trod very warily. Was she, she was certain they wondered inwardly, condemned to the slow march of an inexorable nervous disease that would – in ten or twenty years – confine her to a wheelchair and total dependence on others? Or was she simply a self-centred, neurotic young girl, suffering bouts of imaginary illness at the approach of final examinations? She never knew which of these alternatives she feared more.

All this made her grumpy with Leo. 'Not so bad,' she muttered grudgingly, avoiding his eye.

Sophie could have slaughtered her. Just when she wanted her to make a good impression, she had to start behaving like some teenage dropout.

Leo, though, read Judith clearly. He thought he'd have felt very much the same if he'd been in her shoes. To be the object of everyone's pitying interest must be hard to bear. He'd behaved as badly as any of them, himself. His enquiry, as Judith had obviously spotted, had been little more than a formality. It was his duty, as her father's friend, to ask about her health, and he'd duly asked. She'd found his remark tiresome, and no wonder. It was his own fault. By now he ought to have learnt not to make meaningless gestures aimed vaguely in the direction of a living human being. If he was neither interested in her as a person, nor concerned in any way in her treatment, he should have left her to her privacy.

Nothing he'd have liked better, of course. He was tired after his list, which had gone on well into the middle of the afternoon, so that he'd missed lunch. What he wanted most was peace and quiet, a chance to sit down in his room, sign his letters, and swallow gallons of the strong restorative tea Sophie made. Have a breather.

After all, though, this was Rob's daughter. He pulled himself together. 'What exactly are you doing now?' he asked.

'Nothing much.' The grey eyes were as cold and blank as Rob's own.

Nothing much. Leo's heart bled for her. She must have expected to be qualifying as a physiotherapist by now, and finding her first post. Instead, she was kicking her heels at home, her future problematical.

No wonder she was scratchy. If only he knew her diagnosis, he'd have some grasp of her prospects. But Rob had been evasive, had turned enquiries aside as touchily as his daughter was doing now. He'd talked about no more physiotherapy for a bit, taking things easily for a while instead, and reassessment in six months, perhaps. More than this he'd failed to divulge.

Sophie, watching Leo, reluctantly decided against postponing her plan. Now or never. Probably, she thought irritably, never, as Judith seemed to be set on putting herself in the worst light possible. But Sophie was well aware that if she allowed this opportunity to slip by, raising the issue a day or two later would seem odd. It was not easy to deceive Leo – he'd undoubtedly recollect today's meeting, realise she could have spoken out now, and recognise, too, exactly why she hadn't done so. She'd waited to get him into a more auspicious frame of mind, waited for the memory of Judith's brusqueness to fade. Right. Jump in at the deep end, and Judith had only herself to blame if Leo wouldn't wear the proposal. Serve her right.

'Judith has time on her hands, at present,' she began. 'That's why I asked her to come round. I thought she might be able to give us some help with the follow-up paper for the *Quarterly Review*.'

'With the paper?' Leo was surprised. 'How? Can you type?'

'Oh, yes, I can *type*.' Judith was quelling.

Sophie looked at her with a good deal of exasperation. Nothing was more maddening than to evolve a scheme to help someone, to go to considerable lengths thinking out how best to put it into practice, to spend more time pondering the best way of selling the plan to Leo, only to be thwarted not by him but by her protégée. Of course, Judith had been ill and was still worried about her own future, and this probably accounted for her present awkward behaviour. However, if her temper was going to be as unpredictable as this, perhaps they'd be better off without her.

She needed a regular occupation, though, to tide her over. Sophie was sure of this, and Judith had said she'd like the job. She'd told Sophie she was going quietly mad at home – her only visits to the physiotherapy department now were for treatment, not training at all. And Robert Chasemore, Sophie guessed, was not much help. No one could possibly describe him as outgoing or brimming with ideas and optimism. Whereas Leo possessed exactly those qualities – with him around in her life, Judith would find it difficult to sit back and be miserable. So why couldn't she at least be polite to him?

One more try, Sophie decided, and after that she'd wash her hands of Judith Chasemore. She could go to hell in her own way and bad luck to her.

'Judith keeps her father's records for him – has done for years. Isn't that so?'

'Since I was about fourteen.'

That must have been Judith's age, Leo remembered, when her mother Daphne had gone to America as a member of the team accompanying the heart surgeon, Marcus Northiam.

Judith had been at a London day school, and although panicked by her mother's departure, she'd been excited by the responsibilities that came her way as a result. Proudly, she'd seen herself as her father's new partner, managing his office and running the flat. However, as the Chasemores already had an excellent housekeeper, to whom Daphne had allowed a fairly free hand, Judith's intrusion into domestic affairs led to friction, and to keep the peace, Rob encouraged his over-eager daughter to help him with his office work more and more. She had begun by filing his notes and correspondence, and at odd moments had practised typing on the portable he and Daphne kept in the flat and used to tap out lecture notes and drafts for papers to the journals. When the Easter holidays came Judith had taken a crash course in typing, and since then her father had put his notes on tape for her to type out.

Some of this she related to Leo, in an offhand, abrupt manner that made Sophie want to shake her. Instead, she kept her head – a habit of hers – and set out to explain to Leo what she had in mind. As he already knew, she had been finding it difficult, with his other work, to find the opportunity to organise and type out the material for the five-year follow-up article he and Nick were preparing for the *Quarterly Review of Surgery*. This was what she thought might be handed over to Judith.

Leo listened, nodding now and again, while he continued to watch Judith, thinking quite as much about her unknown diagnosis as about the paper for the *Quarterly Review*. And then, he asked himself, what would Rob have to say about this plan for his daughter to work part-time for him in Harley Street?

Leo was struck by her extraordinary physical resemblance to her father. Now that he knew who she was, he couldn't imagine how he had failed to grasp, the minute he set on eyes on her, that she was Rob's daughter. They shared the same pale, oval face with wide-set grey eyes, the same infuriating remoteness, an air of keeping themselves to themselves and parting with the bare minimum of information consistent with civility. Judith had her mother's chestnut hair, though, together with a hint of humour that certainly didn't come from Rob, who always took himself and the world about him with intense seriousness. But as Leo talked to Judith, a glint of humorous understanding surfaced more than once in the grey eyes and gave her a warmth quite different from Rob's own cool detachment.

Somehow, without knowing quite how he had reached a decision or why, Leo heard himself assenting to the project. Judith should begin work on the paper. Sophie would show her the rough draft, the tables and the case histories, she could get them into order and begin typing.

'All right?' he asked.

'I suppose so,' she responded cagily. And then it happened. Her sense of humour at last made itself heard and succeeded in communicating with her more anxious self. She was being more than a little difficult, to say the least. Downright infuriating, in fact. She saw herself at last through Sophie's exasperated eyes and realised that both Sophie and Leo himself had been trying hard, putting themselves out to handle her and her abominable temperament, while all she had done herself was to keep behaving like a problem child.

She was ashamed of herself. She'd been impossible, snapping their heads off for no reason. As they would have said in the wards, she was not being very co-operative – a damning indictment. She had to smile, though a little sarcastically, at her own cretinous behaviour. 'Sorry,' she told Leo hastily. 'I'm being awful. The job's very much all right, and I'm grateful for it.' She gave him a swift transforming smile that made him momentarily forget about Rob in the background. Then, to his intense surprise and Sophie's unbounded relief, she showed what to him was an invaluable quality – an acute awareness of the passage of time. 'You must be wanting to sign your letters and hear about your messages from Sophie,' she said apologetically. 'I've been taking up far too much of your afternoon. I'll give you a ring, Sophie, to fix a date when I can start.' She looked directly at Leo again. 'Thanks for the job,' she said. 'I'll try and do it nearly as well as Sophie would.' A shade of self-mockery crept into her eyes again, and quirked her mouth at the corners, so that once again she seemed quite unlike her father after all. She crossed the room with fair speed, but with an unmistakable hesitation in her walk that made Leo frown. The door closed behind her. She was gone.

For once Sophie misunderstood the frown. 'I think she'll be all right, you know,' she assured him.

'Oh, yeah, I dare say.' He brought his mind firmly back into the big front room that had once been Lord Mummery's. For some reason, until Sophie spoke, it had been out in the hall with that slender, limping girl, her haunting beauty so oddly echoing her father's mundane appearance that was so familiar to him, and yet so totally different.

'The thing is, it's hopeless for her morale to be cooped up in that flat day after day, with only the housekeeper and her father for company. It'll be so good for her to come across here and get into a different atmosphere – have other people to think about, too.'

Leo's dark eyes glinted. 'Gotta feeling, Soph, you're up to something. Managing me again.'

Sophie evaded his eye. 'It will inconvenience me if anyone,' was all she said. 'Not you. I shall be the one to have her around, explain everything to her, deal with her low morale – and I'll check her stuff for you, so you needn't be afraid you'll be landed with a load of rubbish. Not that I think you would be, in any case. After all, she's been more or less raised at the Central.'

'All right, Soph, I've agreed. I shan't back out.' No one but Leo ever called Sophie by this version of her name, but over the years the abbreviation had become almost an endearment, and Sophie smiled ravishingly at him. 'So 'ow about a cuppa char?' he demanded, cashing in at once.

'Coming up,' she told him.

He drank the strong tea thankfully, signed his letters, dictated a fresh batch, and made a few telephone calls. After this he rang intensive care for a report on that day's patients, heard they were all, even Miss Kilpatrick, coming along nicely, and went off to his flat to change and go out with Melanie, the actress they'd been discussing before his arrival that morning.

About midnight he returned, and heard the telephone ringing as he unlocked the front door.

Robert Chasemore was on the line. 'Miss Kilpatrick, who was making a good recovery,' he said, his voice sombre, 'has just died suddenly. It must have been a massive embolus.'

'When?'

'Less than half an hour ago. I'm sorry.'

'I see.'

'Thought you'd want to be informed.'

'Yes. Thanks very much, Rob.'

'All for the best, I dare say. In view of what you found.'

'Suppose so. Thanks, anyway.' He put the telephone down. Rob was right, it had been a merciful end, all things considered. But he felt horrible.

He roamed his colourful flat — he had red carpets, red velvet curtains, in the passages even red-striped wallpaper — and tried to come to terms with Miss Kilpatrick's loss. It was only, he reminded himself, what she herself would have wished. Her future had been bleak. She had no more to live for, she was ready to go. She'd told him so.

So was it no more than his own pride that was hurt? A dislike of letting any patient under his personal care be so presumptuous as to die on him?

He shook his head. Nothing so simple. He was saddened by her death. An old friend had gone. He'd never see her again, never look into those bright, resolutely cheerful old eyes, never again have one of his invigorating chats with her. She had gone. He'd spoken to her last night, but now she was gone, her spirit had departed. She'd given her body into his care four or five years ago, but he'd failed to look after it well enough. Failed to keep her alive. Failed, even, to keep her out of pain. What was more, if he hadn't interfered, hadn't decided to open her up this morning, she'd be alive now. In pain, but alive.

He opened the window, and leaned out into the night air of the city, heavy still with the smell of petrol and diesel mingled with curry from the Indian restaurant round the corner and pungent clarifying fat from the basement of the hotel on the other corner. Public houses had emptied but there were still a few drunks about shouting occasionally, and cars revving now and again.

London never slept.

As usual, though, the bustle and the noise reassured him. Life went on, tomorrow would dawn and work would go on. He stretched, said a swift and secret prayer for the safe passage of Miss Kilpatrick's soul, and went to bed.

And to sleep. And the last face he saw before he drifted off was not that of old Miss Kilpatrick after all, but Judith Chasemore. The dead had no further need of him, but the living still required his care, and he had an uneasy suspicion that Judith had a hard road ahead of her.

# Chapter 3

The next morning when he awoke, Leo found he was still thinking about Judith. He remembered, too, himself at the opening of his final year as a medical student, the hopefulness that had both possessed and driven him – and the immense surging energy that had ridden him day and night. It was this that had led him to walk the wards, to watch surgery from early until late, and to attend every lecture and demonstration he could somehow or other fit in. The textbooks and monographs he'd devoured – now helping to fill the loaded bookshelves in his flat – into the small hours.

What would he have felt if suddenly this had been snatched away? If he'd been informed, after an odd bizarre experience that had then evaporated apparently into nothing, like an early morning mist, that he was not fit enough to continue?

He'd have fought the decision. The answer came to him with absolute certainty. He'd have fought it and altered it.

Did this account, more than the unknown diagnosis, for Judith's snappiness yesterday afternoon? Was she, perhaps, refusing to accept both the regime and the interruption to her studies prescribed for her? But then she wasn't a medical student. Physiotherapy was different – impossible to continue in it without exceptionally robust physical health.

Brooding over the problem, he plugged in his machine for making coffee and began on the huge breakfast that years of surgery had taught him to get inside himself at the start of the day – it could easily be not only his first but his last meal, followed by endless cups of tea or coffee, tubs of yoghurt or packets of canteen sandwiches.

If Judith needed a helping hand, he told himself surprisingly fiercely, as he demolished a mountain of hot toast and kipper pâté, he'd be right there beside her, battling on her behalf.

He pulled himself up short. He couldn't be. Anything of this sort would be not only unjustifiable interference but highly irresponsible, too. What had come over him? Why was he possessed by this urgent need to stand shoulder to shoulder with this difficult girl, fighting her battles for her? She was neither his patient nor his relative, she wasn't on his staff and, what was more, she'd given every sign of being entirely capable of looking after herself. And Rob Chasemore was her father. If she needed help from anyone, Rob was there to provide it.

He sighed. Rob was a capable physician, but reassurance had never been among his strong points. If Judith's illness, whatever it was, was going to halt her training, prevent her from qualifying and working as a physiotherapist in the wards, she needed support. And he might not be capable of giving it to her.

Exactly what was the picture regarding her health, then? He'd have to have a talk with Rob about it. Apart from anything else, he'd need to know if she was going to be working for him.

First of all, he decided, he'd check with Professor Collingham. He knew Rob had referred his daughter to the eminent neurologist for his opinion. Later on that morning he tracked Collingham down in his office in the department of neurology. 'Wonder if we could have a brief word? About Judith Chasemore – she's proposing to do some work for me, in Harley Street. Office work, not as a physio. But I was wondering what exactly she's fit to take on. If she needs watching at all, that sort of thing?'

Professor Collingham, thin and greying, leant back in his chair, and his alert eyes met Leo's. 'Glad you asked me,' he said. 'Frankly, Judith Chasemore worries me.'

The two of them talked for nearly half an hour, which was by their standards a long time. Afterwards Leo walked thoughtfully back to his own office in general surgery, picked up the telephone, and rang Rob. 'Care to come over for a bite this evening, Rob? Matter I wanted to discuss.'

Rob said he was free, and they fixed a time. As Leo put the telephone down he realised that since he'd said nothing about Judith, Rob would be assuming this would simply be one of their routine chats about a problem case. 'Another tricky gas, he must suppose I want him for,' he reflected. 'Not a tricky point about his own daughter.'

He was right. Slim and smoothly tailored in a suit that had undoubtedly not come off a rack in any chain store, Rob came confidently into the flat with no inkling that this meeting was anything more than one of their usual pre-operative discussions.

'Sorry, Rob.' Leo handed over a more than usually potent mixture – and he was famous for mixing strong drinks – in one of his heavy cut-glass tumblers. 'Got something to say y'may not care for.' Professor Collingham had warned him he'd find Chasemore difficult to handle on the subject of Judith.

'Strong resistance to admitting the diagnosis,' the professor had told Leo. 'Seems to think if he doesn't look it in the face it'll somehow go away. None of us have been able to get through this barrier. He won't have the girl told, either, which we feel is quite wrong. Be relieved if you'd take a hand, try to make him see sense. He might listen to you, where he hasn't to us.'

'I doubt it.'

'People have been known to – can't imagine why.' Collingham's rare and wintry smile had gleamed for a short frosty moment. 'Anyway, we think it's important the girl should be made aware of her own likely diagnosis. She's a physio – or she was – and she ought to be told. Face up to her own future. Physiotherapy is the last occupation for a girl with her history. She can't go on with it. So she ought to know where she stands – after all, there are plenty of other jobs she could do. The sooner she and that obstinate father of hers face reality the better.'

'I'll have a go at Rob,' Leo had promised.

However, ensconced on Leo's vast black leather chesterfield in his neat pinstripe, Rob was difficult to deal with.

'What I wanted to talk about this evening is Judith.'

'Judy?' Rob was momentarily startled, but then he recollected his daughter's remarks at breakfast that morning. 'Oh, yes,' he agreed amicably, 'she said she was going to do some clerical work for you round in Harley Street. Well, I've nothing against it. Go ahead and use her – that's no problem. Kind of you to think of her – she's at a bit of a loose end just now, I'm afraid.'

A bit of a loose end. Leo could have sworn at Rob as colourfully as his grandfather might have done in the old market days. Instead, he sat down very deliberately in the leather armchair that he bought on his appointment as a consultant at the Central, raised his surprisingly small, neat feet to its matching footstool, took a cautious drink of his whisky, and leant back. Surveying the ceiling inscrutably, he remarked, 'Bit of an understatement, that, wouldn't you say?' His voice, though he was quite unaware of this, had shed most of its cockney vigour and become flatly neutral, almost as academic as Professor Collingham's.

'Understatement?' Rob was plainly puzzled. 'Well, she does a certain amount of clerical work for me, you know. And she reads a lot. But it's not the routine she's used to, of course.'

'But you can't expect her to go on like that indefinitely.'

Rob shrugged, his cool grey eyes at their most blank and unreadable. 'It's not for ever,' he pointed out. 'Only a question of a month or two. Just until she's fully fit again. I don't for a minute suppose she'll have a recurrence. It was simply an odd little episode she had.'

'Rob.' The word erupted from Leo as he put his feet back on the red carpet with a force that sent the footstool swivelling madly on its stainless steel base. 'I warned you. You won't like what I'm going to say. So here it is. It wasn't an odd little episode. There were two of them and that makes it a hell of a lot more serious. And you know it.'

'Really, you know, there's not the slightest necessity for all this concern, either on your part or Collingham's. Judith and I – '

'Are sticking y'r heads into the sand like a couple of bleeding ostriches. And she's going to be the one to suffer. Not you.'

'Oh, no. She shan't suffer, I swear it. Not through any neglect of mine.'

Leo had got through Rob's defences.

'I shan't let her suffer,' he told Leo. And now his tone was anguished.

'Look, mate, you can look after her, all right. No one, least of all me, is going to dispute that. You can care for her and see she gets the right treatment. But you've no right to keep her in the dark about what's going on. You mustn't do it. Let the girl know what she's up against.'

Chasemore's eyes at last met Leo's, and for a split second naked fear stared out at him. Then it was gone, and the eyes went blank again. 'What are you trying to tell me, Leo? Judy's going to get better. She's going to be all right. There won't be any recurrence.' Rob spoke faster than usual, and his knuckles showed white as he clenched his hands into fists. 'Judith's had perfect health up to now.'

'Until now, that's right. Face it, Rob. This is serious. You can't turn your back on it. Judith's only got you to turn to, and it seems to me you've no right to conceal the diagnosis – all right then, the probable diagnosis, if that's the way you want it – but at least *tell* her. She's not a child. Pull yourself together and be straight with her.'

'I suppose I've been funking it.' A big admission for anyone like Rob. 'Can't really face it myself, you see.' He was being totally honest now, though his face remained schooled and his expression blank. 'It came just like that one day, out of a clear sky. We were playing tennis – she was partnering me in the hospitals tournament, and she started missing balls. I thought it was an attack of nerves, but afterwards she told me she'd started seeing double, so I sent her to Dovercourt.' This was the senior eye specialist at the Central.

'What did he say?'

'I was hoping, you see, that it still might be no more than nerves or, alternatively, perhaps a lazy eye.'

"What did Dovercourt think?" Leo tried the question a second time, in a different form.

'He said it wasn't a lazy eye. There was a central vision defect.' Rob ground the words out unwillingly. 'He recommended I asked Collingham to see her as well.'

'He was already thinking of multiple sclerosis, in fact?'

Rob drank some whisky. 'Well, yes, he was,' he had to admit. 'But I didn't at that stage necessarily accept it. And when Collingham saw her, all he said was wait and see.' Rob shot what could only be a triumphant glance at Leo, as though he'd won an argument, and that was that. An end to the discussion.

'And then she had another episode,' Leo reminded him.

'Yes, I suppose she did.' Rob had recourse to his whisky again.

'Suppose? You know damn well she did. Pull yourself together, Rob. Stop hedging and face reality.'

Rob frowned. 'I know now, shall we say? But at the time it seemed nothing.'

'What actually happened?'

'She'd been writing letters – in her room, sitting at her desk, and she found when she came to get up that her foot seemed to have gone to sleep. Or so she imagined. She didn't even tell me that night. Just went to bed.'

'And in the morning?'

'The foot was still affected. Like pins and needles, she said, and it was numb, too. I don't know that she would have told me even then, but she tripped getting up from the breakfast table, and so the story came out.' He gulped some whisky. 'I didn't know what to tell her.' His voice shook slightly. 'I couldn't blurt out that I thought this second occurrence, added to the earlier double-vision as it was, made Dovecourt's original diagnosis correct. But of course I knew it did. I hardly needed to send her to Collingham, I was so sure.'

'Though in fact you did.'

'Yes.'

'And he confirmed your own opinion.' At least, Leo thought, they had reached a point where Rob himself had ceased to deny the obvious.

'Yes. There's nothing to be gained by telling her, though, as far as I can see. After all, she might easily have twenty or twenty-five years ahead of her before she gets another episode. Or she may never have another symptom.'

'She still has the weakness in the right foot. I've watched her.'

'Yes. But she may soon be rid of that, with plenty of physiotherapy.'

'Then there's this problem of her career. What are you proposing to do about that? Collingham doesn't think she can continue in physiotherapy. Physically, it's about the hardest job there is around a hospital, I would have thought.'

'But the hours are regular. No broken nights. And looking after patients once you're qualified is by no means as strenuous as training. She'll have to have some sort of break, of course. That's why I'm glad she's going to do this work for you. She can fill in time, exercise that weak leg, and then perhaps next year, with a little understanding from the authorities, I don't see why she shouldn't complete her training and qualify.'

'I think you're asking a lot. And it seems to me she herself ought to be the judge of whether she ought to take on such a stiff programme.'

Rob sighed, and drained his glass. 'I can't help it. I simply don't know how in the world I'm going to spell it out to her.' He took the refilled glass Leo handed him without apparently noticing. 'Hell,' he said bitterly, 'why did this have to happen to her, of all people? To Judy?'

Leo, watching him, understood that he was suffering much more than he or Collingham had realised. In daily life Robert Chasemore was such a cold fish that to find that anyone meant as much to him as Judith obviously did was a shock.

'She's our only child, all that's left of our marriage,' he was saying. 'Up to now everything seemed set fair for her. She was doing well in her training, she was enjoying herself, and — and really she seemed exceptionally fit. I never for a second imagined anything like this. She's always played a lot of tennis, and she swims most days, too. Or she used to.' He stared into his whisky, brooding.

He was thinking about his marriage, Leo decided. He remembered that when Daphne Chasemore had been at the Central, she and Rob had been enthusiastic tennis players, representing the hospital all over the country. Leo himself had throughout his life been the reverse of athletic, and he'd never felt any urge to watch tennis, rugger or rowing, but he recollected hearing that Judith Chasemore had become as good a tennis player as her mother, and that she now partnered Rob in matches. Well, Rob would have to pull himself together and find another partner, he thought unsympathetically.

'You've got to tell the girl what she may be facing, not allow her to drift along for months on end doing nothing in particular and feeling miserable.'

'I have discussed it with her,' Rob said obstinately. 'And I've advised her to follow a régime with which Collingham's in entire agreement, so why in the world should she be made miserable and unhappy by being confronted with the worst prognosis we can lay our hands on?'

'If I were in her shoes, I'd want to know where I stood. Make my own decisions. Fight my own way through it.' Leo, in his turn, was obstinate.

'But you aren't in her shoes, Leo. She's a young girl of twenty – '

'Not an old man of nearly forty?' For some reason he couldn't fathom he was furious with Rob, would have liked to have knocked him flat on to the Turkey carpet. Instead, he lay back in his chair, regarded his whisky with more concentration than usual, and remarked only, 'If I was twenty, though, I'd still want to know. And I wouldn't consider anyone, whether in my family or in the department of neurology, had the right to hide any possible diagnosis from me.'

Rob drank off the rest of his whisky, and said, sombrely, 'I can't do it, Leo. I simply cannot spell out the future I see for her if Collingham's view should be correct. And there it is. It may be a failure on my part. I accept that. But I can't do it.'

'I can understand your feelings. But at least give Collingham the go-ahead.'

'No.' The word exploded into the room. 'I won't have it. Judy's not going to have a foretaste of doom

spelled out with cold precision by that machine of a
neurologist. Would you want anyone in your family
dealt a life sentence by a computer?'

'He's not an inhuman monster. If you won't tell her,
someone's got to.'

'The moment she's told, whoever breaks the news,
she's going to work out all the implications for herself.
That's why I don't want her to know. Why should she
have to suffer like that? Time enough.'

'Can't you see she may be made far more anxious
by not knowing?'

'No. I can't. No news is good news, after all. And it
isn't as if anyone had any certainty to offer her.
Suppose she has no more symptoms at all for twenty
years?'

Leo sighed. 'It's up to you, Rob. But at least talk to
her about it, won't you?'

'Oh, I'll talk to her. But not in the way you and
Collingham would like.'

'You put me in a difficult position.'

'You? Why? I fail to see where you come into this.'
Rob was irritable.

'She's going to be working for me, remember? So
what am I supposed to say if she starts asking me
questions, eh? Tell her a load of lies? Not on, Rob. I
won't do it.'

Rob looked hunted. 'If she asks you anything, you
can tell her the truth,' he said. 'I wouldn't mind her
hearing it from you, if she has to hear it from someone.
But no need to go out of your way. Right? It seems
extremely unlikely to me that she'll ask you anything.'

'But if she does, I have your permission to explain
the true position to her?'

'Naturally.'

'All right. That's understood, then. And as you say,

I doubt if it'll arise – so I do wish you'd see your way to having a good talk with her yourself. In depth, as they say.'

'I'll think about it,' Rob promised.

Leo had little hope that anything would come of this. The ball was back in his court, he reflected a trifle sardonically. All he'd achieved, by having this talk with Rob, was to land himself with the hard decision of how much to tell Judith Chasemore about her illness and her future.

# Chapter 4

In general surgery, where the surveillance system was of a standard that might have been envied by any dictatorship, they were aware almost to the minute when 'that actress of Leo's' flew out of Heathrow en route for New York. So now what, they asked one another?

Leo was asking himself the same question. His affair with Melanie had lasted over five years. Before she'd left, though, she'd said goodbye very firmly.

'Perhaps it's just as well I'm going to New York, darling. I'm getting too fond of you. If we go on like this, one of these days I might be idiot enough to throw over my career and start raising little Rosensteins.'

'You'd never want to do that,' he said hastily, to her mingled disappointment and relief. Well as she knew him, she couldn't make out what his rapid disclaimer covered. Did he mean he himself would hate it, or had he been secretly longing for her to respond by flinging her arms around him, assuring him that that and nothing else was what she wanted in life? Over the years they'd spent together, she'd found out that he was much more sensitive and unsure of himself than anyone could have guessed. It was possible – but only just – that while he'd carry her to bed and make love with confidence, he'd be plain shy of asking her to give up acting to settle down with him.

In fact, he didn't know the answer himself. After she'd gone, he missed her, was far more lonely than he'd been prepared for. He took to spending more evenings than usual upstairs in Harley Street with Nick and Sophie. Once or twice he took Sister Henderson out, too, and brought her up to date with what was going on in general surgery since she'd left.

The hospital, not for the first occasion, jumped instantly to the wrong conclusion, adding two and two and making twenty-two. Melanie had gone. Leo was finished with actresses. Now that Sister Henderson was no longer at his beck and call night and day in the theatre, he had at last realised how much she meant to him. He was finally going to settle down, and he'd not be the first philandering surgeon to end up marrying his theatre sister, would he?

In the general surgery theatre they were agog. Stella Jarvis, who as his present theatre sister had been informed by everyone of all the details of her new chief's love life, real and imaginary, past and current, as recorded in the department hour by hour, almost, handed him instruments and asked herself if this amazing man – a surgeon whose skill she admired immensely, which was saying a good deal for someone coming from neurosurgery, as she did, and whose personality made an impact wherever he went (rooms vibrated round him, and not simply because he was big-boned and overweight) – could this larger-than-life character be going after all to settle tamely down to wedded bliss with someone as ordinary as Sister Henderson?

She found herself, to her consternation, fervently praying that he wouldn't. She was shocked at her reaction. She was fond of Barbie Henderson, liked her – owed her this job, too.

And then what about Larry? She couldn't be over him so easily, surely? She'd loved him to distraction for years, and she was grieving still for the gap his absence left in her life. She longed for him, if not night and day – no theatre sister at the Central had overmuch spare time for longing for anyone – certainly for any waking part of her nights. She couldn't have put him behind her already. Yet now, in the general theatre, opposite the burly, green-gowned figure of her present chief, she'd undoubtedly been hoping he surely wasn't going to marry boring Sister Henderson when she, exciting Sister Jarvis, was available.

Her brown eyes, larger than ever with this unbidden sexual excitement, met his as she handed him the retractors. He was intrigued. So this new theatre sister of his was beginning to fancy him, was she?

'Doing anything tonight, Sister?' he enquired.

The entire theatre stiffened to attention. Eyes crossed.

'Because I've a couple of tickets for the Tchaikovsky concert at the Festival Hall, if you'd care to join me. Or is Tchaikovsky too lush f'you?'

'No way.' Her liquid brown eyes met his again. 'Tchaikovsky is meat and drink to me, you might say.' She took a deep breath of delight. 'I think he's the greatest.' Her eyes were soft now, soft and , the theatre considered, romantic. But were all these emotions for Tchaikovsky or Leo?

'We'll go, then.' Leo was brisk. 'Meet me in the King's Head, right?' He had not spent nearly twenty years of his life at the Central without learning to read their hearts and minds, often long before they read them themselves, and he wasn't going to give any of these avid ear-flapping staff of his the satisfaction of hearing him make a date with her at either of their flats. In any case, he had a strong sense of self-preservation. A meal and a concert committed no one to anything, and he'd have an opportunity to find out what she was like off-duty.

What she was like was beautiful. Amazingly beautiful. When she walked into the King's Head to meet him she'd had time to change, and looked entirely delectable, he thought, in a creamy silk knitted suit that clung to her slim figure.

All he said was 'What'll you drink? And can you exist on a couple of hot sausages and a hunk of bread and cheese? Because we haven't too much time. We'll have a meal after the concert.'

'That'd be great,' she said, relaxed and easy. Or so at any rate she appeared to the housemen and registrars downing beer at the bar and surveying the encounter. 'Could I have a lager to go with the sausages?'

'Sure that'll do you? Wouldn't like gin, whisky, rum?'

'I dare say I could have a rum and coke later?' she suggested. 'With this meal you mentioned. Just now I'm mainly thirsty.'

'Right. Lager it is. Coming up.' He shouldered his way through the crowd round the bar, leaving her at the small table he'd been keeping. Stella looked round, waved to a few friends, and wondered if Larry would come in. And if he did, what would she feel? Did she want him to see her with Leo, having an evening out, or would she be panicked? More to the point, would he be panicked? And if he was, so what?

She sat at Leo's side through the surging Tchaikovsky, remembering Larry and telling herself she needed her head examining.

Afterwards, when they were seated at a table in the

restaurant he took her to – an obviously expensive place in St James's that she'd never entered before – he looked into her brown eyes and saw at once that they were no longer sexy or inviting. Simply sad.

'Tchaikovsky make you miserable?' he demanded, not being a man to dodge any obstacles he came across in his path.

'Yes,' she agreed, her wide smile gentle now, her brows rising a little ironically into two dark arcs of self-mockery. 'I'm afraid he did.' She picked up the glass of cold, refreshing Chablis he'd chosen, and sipped it. 'Perhaps I'm just hungry and a bit tired,' she said apologetically. This was no way to behave when the fascinating Leo Rosenstein, her chief, dated her for the first time. She had to pull herself together, be entertaining and a good companion as well as seductive. She had heavy competition. Not only that string of actresses, but Sister Henderson, too. And placid, boring Sister Henderson, he'd soon be thinking, would have been a better dinner partner than jumpy, neurotic Stella Jarvis, who'd turned out to be a right misery.

'No good trying to fob me off,' he told her. 'Never works. People try it from time to time, but I never wear it. Come clean, duckie.'

So she came clean. 'I'm afraid I was thinking about Larry,' she said in a small, frightened voice. She gulped her wine hastily. She must be bonkers. Or was she? She was in enough of a muddle already, and to try to deceive Leo would probably be more than she could handle – entrancing as the prospect of becoming one of his girl friends had seemed at a distance. She sighed, wishing she was some *femme fatale*. Not a hope. She was just Leo's very ordinary and ludicrously honest theatre sister.

'Larry?' he asked. He'd heard the gossip, of course. Silly to pretend he didn't know what she was talking about. 'Laurence Bridge, that would be,' he said firmly.

She nodded, her eyes anxious now, and drank more Chablis.

'Registrar in neurosurgery. You lived with him until recently, so they say. That right?'

She nodded again. What a way to handle her first – and no doubt last – evening with Leo.

He grinned cheerfully at her. 'No need to look as if I'm gonna rape you on the spot, to pay you out for mentioning him.' He drank some wine himself, though. Suddenly the evening was turning out to be entirely different from what he'd expected. Stella Jarvis was a beautiful and fashionable lady, but the packaging was deceptive. Fascinating she remained, but she was also forlorn, eating her heart out for Lawrence Bridge still. A loving and faithful girl. So what was he, Leo Rosenstein, going to do about her? Was he going to pick her up and force her into forgetting that neurosurgical registrar, make her notice him instead? Or was he going to sit back, mop her up, and let her work her own life out for herself? He was undecided.

'Better tell me about him,' he said casually, turning his attention, as far as she could see, to his smoked trout.

She picked up her own fork, and began to spear scampi. 'Tell – tell you about him?' She sounded like a scared fourteen-year-old up before the head.

'That's right.' He followed a mouthful of trout with another of brown bread and butter, folded in half. 'No,' he added suddenly. 'Don't. Maybe you're right. Maybe you're hungry, like you said. Eat up, and when we've both got a square meal inside us, we'll talk about Larry.' He couldn't quite stop himself in time from pronouncing the name distastefully.

Stella caught her breath. 'I'm sorry,' she said. 'It's awful of me to keep on about him.'

Yes, he thought belligerently. It is awful of you. No girl in her right mind should have the nerve to look across at me the way you did in the theatre earlier today, and then come along and sit opposite me here bleating away about her lost Larry. However, he reminded himself, he'd always been a soft-hearted idiot. What was more, he wasn't any longer a jealous, insecure young house surgeon, ready to take offence if a bird failed to fall straight into his arms with little squeaks of excitement and joy. Besides, what had he to be jealous about? He'd only asked Stella out as an experiment. Like a good deal of research, it turned out to have unforeseen results.

They talked surgery until the end of the meal, but then, with coffee in front of them, he returned to Lawrence Bridge.

'Now,' he said. 'Shoot. First of all, what made you separate? Lot of people seemed to expect you to marry the guy, not leave 'im.'

Stella pulled at her long, brown fingers. 'The old story,' she told him. 'Marriage or career.'

'Both being impossible for some reason?'

'Oh, yes. Everyone told me I had to choose. All my set were sisters, and there was me, still a staff nurse. And I knew exactly why. My time-keeping was terrible, and I couldn't give my mind to my job.'

'OK. So you couldn't do both. Why not marriage? If you say you love the bloke.'

'That's what Larry wanted to know.' She twisted her hands furiously. 'But, Leo, I want to be a nursing sister. That's what I trained for. Not a housewife shut away in a tiny house in the suburbs. Away from all the action.'

'What's wrong with a flat near the hospital?'

'That's what I said. It wasn't my idea to split up. My plan was for us both to move into a modern flat, easy to run and round the corner from the Central. I could have coped then.'

'Weren't you coping before?'

'No.' She shook her head dismally. 'That little house was too far out, and murder to run. But Larry loves it – more than he does me, I suppose that's what I've learnt. Anyway, there he is, still in it, and I'm in a nice new flat all by myself.'

'Sounds like a picture of two obstinate characters.'

'Oh, do you think so?' Clearly she hadn't seen it like that before.

'As you've just said yourself. He's putting the 'ouse first. You're putting the job first. One of you has got to give.'

She shook her head. 'Well,' she was on the defensive, 'I couldn't have gone on like that. I was tearing myself apart trying to be two people at once.' She smiled. It was a wide, sad smile, once again not sexy at all, and it filled Leo with mingled pain and irritation.

What was he doing here, listening to all this at the end of a hard day?

'So now,' she went on, 'I'm still tearing myself apart, asking myself if I've ruined my life simply for the sake of being a career person when I'm not one at all. I feel dreadful. I've got my lovely new flat, and I hate it.' She stared balefully into space, and drank her coffee. He refilled her cup. 'I'm so sorry,' she said, her eyes focusing on him again. 'Here I am, working in the theatre in this job I was longing for, and all I do is moan. I shouldn't bore you with all this stuff about my idiotic muddles – and, anyway, it isn't that I'm not happy in the job. That's the one part of my life that's a success. I enjoy every minute. I find working in the theatre absorbing.'

He nodded. 'So do I. Even so, satisfying work isn't the whole story of anyone's life. You're lonely without Larry. That's the problem.' He looked back into the past, and remembered his own acute loneliness when Jane Drummond had married Michael Adversane and left the Central. It hadn't occurred to him to go chasing after her – much good it would have done him if he had, she had been well and truly in love with Michael, and still was – but without her the hospital had turned into a desert, and the years had stretched bleakly ahead. But, he realised, looking back along them, they hadn't been bleak when he came to live them. Though so far he'd never found anyone to stir him as Jane had done. On one point, though, he had no doubts. 'Takes a hell of a while to get over the love of your life,' he told Stella. He meant it as comfort.

'Oh, Leo, I do miss him so terribly.' The great brown eyes swam mistily, and she looked more amazingly beautiful than ever. Intensely aware of her need, Leo leaned across the table and took her hand for a quick reassuring press. No one, after all, he reminded himself, knew better what she was going through than he did, and it was hell.

She found his warm grip electrifying.

This he didn't for a moment guess – his own sensations being a determined cheerfulness coupled with a mild irritation. Here he'd been, he'd supposed, no Melanie to turn to, but a new and exciting theatre sister ready and waiting to step into the emptiness. He

had been looking forward to the enlivening and
invigorating opening stages of a new and promising
relationship. He'd expected, too, an evening out that
would have allowed him to forget the problems of the
hospital, send him back refreshed to the wards and
clinics and another day's slog.

Instead, this lovely theatre sister of his, with her
exotic looks and her deft touch, was able to dwell on
nothing and nobody but her lost Larry.

He knew Laurence Bridge. A brilliant young man,
and a very able and promising neurosurgeon. He'd go
far in his career, they were all agreed on that, even if
he wasn't the most popular registrar around the hospital. He and Stella had been a spectacularly handsome
pair, Laurence as blond as Stella was dark, a tall man
with, it had to be accepted, a fastidious and slightly
superior attitude to the world about him. Or was he
being hopelessly unfair, Leo wondered, disliking the
man's appearance out of jealousy only? Whatever the
attitude meant, it was easy to credit Stella's claim that
keeping house for Larry was a full-time job,
demanding the same sort of meticulous attention that
she was devoting now to running the general theatre.

To take her over, make her forget Laurence Bridge,
would be much more difficult than he had previously
supposed. So what should he do? Was he going to take
the trouble?

If Melanie had not been in New York, he knew he
would have lost interest long before the end of the
meal. But Melanie was out of reach, and Stella was
here – not only now, opposite him in the restaurant,
but at his side daily in the theatre.

# Chapter 5

At the end of the following day, Leo looked in at Harley Street as usual to sign his letters and collect his messages. His mind, though, seemed not wholly concentrated on them. Sophie, like all his staff, was certain she knew exactly why this was. He was thinking about Stella Jarvis, with whom the hospital was sure he'd embarked on a heady affair. Sophie had her own reasons for being thankful for the distraction.

He signed the final letter, and stretched. 'Are we through?'

'As far as the mail is concerned. But there was something I wanted to ask you.'

'Ask away,' he said airily, not suspecting a thing.

What she had to say succeeding in rocking him.

'I've started a baby,' she announced.

Leo, as Sophie informed Nick at supper later that evening, gulped. 'Truly, he positively gulped. And swallowed, and then it was just as if he'd passed a hand across his face, all expression left it, and then – it's about the only time I've known him to be blatantly insincere – he beamed at me with enormous amiability and said, "Splendid, I'm delighted." Anyone less delighted it's difficult to imagine.'

'So then what?'

'Then I maundered on a bit about how pleased we both were, and how glad we are to be starting our family at last. I wanted to soften him up, make him really frightened about how he was going to manage.

When I thought he'd had about enough, I said, "Now, about your work," and paused, and at once he cottoned on, and so instantaneously he must have picked it out of the air or something, he said, "You've fixed me up, Soph. I might have known you would. Thank God for that. For a minute or two you had me worried." '

Nick laughed. 'You need to rise early to pull one over on our Leo. So how did he take your plan about Judith?'

'Dubiously. At first, anyway. But I kept on pointing out I'd be here at the end of the telephone, and it dawned on him that taking on Judith was a way of keeping me on too, whereas if he had someone from outside he'd hardly be able to do that, so he came round. I assured him she was keen on the idea – if you ask me she's relieved to have an excuse for not trying to go back to her training – '

'She's certainly not robust enough for physiotherapy at present.'

'No, of course she isn't. Luckily, Leo doesn't think she is, either, so he's going to talk to Rob Chasemore, to clear it with him, and then he'll talk to Judith herself. I don't think I'd better let on to her that he's going to approach her father first. She'd be livid. She's terribly fond of him, but she's definitely under the impression she runs her own life.'

Judith, a little to her surprise, was stimulated by the new job, and especially by working for Leo. Her career at a standstill, her future uncertain, stooging for an overweight, uncouth surgeon sprung from a family of greengrocers, typing his letters, making his appointments, driving him here and there and waiting around for him with her little book – she was happier than she'd ever been.

Leo, of course, was enormous fun to be with – that was an unexpected bonus – and, because the routine was still new to her, she found her work stretched her. And it was stimulating, too, to be back, in and out of the hospital with a job to do again, part of everything, without the complication of her uncertain status in physiotherapy – sometimes patient, sometimes student. Her own group had qualified, which made matters more awkward, so that she now evaded going into the physiotherapy department. The students there now were her juniors, and she felt herself unbearably clumsy under their eyes. But as Leo's secretary she was a newcomer, with a useful hospital background, and a limp that was of no importance at all – except, that was, to Leo himself, who tended to bully her about it. Unlike her contemporaries, though, he didn't appear to be in the least sorry for her.

The physiotherapists who'd been students with her, with their new jobs – some of them in the Central – were upset by her new role. She'd come down in the world, as they saw it, in addition to being ill, and when they encountered her they first of all looked aghast and then stopped in their tracks, jettisoning whatever they had been about to do in favour of providing her with the necessary shoulder to lean on, as well as a huge dose of encouragement. Snappily, she would assure them she was doing all right, but this they would brush aside, knowing only too well about the notorious Chasemore reserve and assuming this to be a demonstration of it.

Leo rescued her from one of these unwelcome sessions – she'd seldom been so relieved to see anyone, and her face lit up as he appeared.

He was delighted. 'That's my girl,' he told her. 'I like it when a bird puts up the illuminations for me.'

'Oh, did I?' She was embarrassed.

'Now don't go and spoil it.'

'No, I was tremendously pleased to see you,' she said truthfully. 'They – they're always so *sorry* for me.'

'And I'm not?'

'If you are you keep it to yourself. Are you?'

He was, of course. 'How do you mean?'

'Are you sorry for me? Well?' The clear grey eyes so like Rob's searched his with an appeal he was unable to deny.

'In a way.' He was cautious.

'What way?' She was looking at him, he saw with dismay, with absolute trust, and he knew he was lost. Here it comes, he thought. I'm going to have to tell her, do what Rob should have done months earlier.

'Have they told you your likely diagnosis?' he asked, knowing very well they hadn't.

'No. I couldn't get them to. Talk to your father, they kept saying. Do you know it?'

He wasn't going to lie. 'Yes.'

'There you are.' She almost spat the words at him. 'Everyone but me.'

'I discussed it with your father.'

'And?'

'He – I thought he ought to tell you, and I said so to him. But he said he found it too difficult, and – and he feels there's no purpose in your knowing, anyway.'

'You mean it's nasty, don't you?'

'It isn't good, I'm afraid.' So now he'd committed himself. Hell, though, he couldn't blurt it out here in the corridor, and then walk away, leaving her to recover as best she could from what was bound to be a body blow. 'This isn't the place to go into it.' They'd been standing in the main corridor off the general theatre suites, with all the world passing and repassing round them, traffic coming and going from the anaesthetic room, the changing-rooms, sister's office, the lifts. 'I've a few people I must see in intensive care before I leave the building,' he said. 'So come into the surgeons' rest-room with me, and I'll sign this lot you've got here, and you can get them off.'

She followed him into the room where he, Nick, Jeremy and the house surgeons relaxed and drank tea or coffee between operations. Battered comfortable chairs stood about, stranded in the middle of the floor in curiously unsociable positions, and while Leo signed the pile of letters Judith stared round but saw very little. Was Leo going to talk to her honestly about this illness of hers, discuss it fully, or would he, like everyone else so far, simply slide away from the subject?

He signed the last letter, handed her the pile, and stood up. 'Cope with those, then, while I see this morning's patients in intensive care.'

She waited. Would he or wouldn't he?

He was looking through his notebook. 'Then,' he said, almost absently, turning over pages and scrutinising their entries, 'if you come across to the flat with me, with any luck we can snatch an undisturbed half-hour. We can have a brief session on this problem of yours. OK?'

'Oh, Leo, *thank* you.' She took a breath, and the disconcerting grey eyes searched his.

'It may not – well, won't – make easy hearing,' he warned her.

'If I could just *know*. Where shall I meet you?'

'In the main hall. In, say, half an hour.'

'I'll be there.'

He was punctual, and they walked out through the sliding glass doors together, a big bulky man with a brisk stride and a tawny-haired, frail-looking girl with a hesitation in her walk.

Round the corner to his flat in the old-fashioned block, and up in the rattling lift, so different from the high-speed lifts in the surgical tower.

'Better 'ave a drink,' he announced. He wasn't sure which of them was going to need it most. 'Siddown.'

It wasn't the first time she'd been in his flat, of course, and she sat at once on the black leather settee that had become familiar to her since she'd began attending the pre-list discussions in his sitting-room with Jeremy and his house surgeon and, often, Stella – though then they normally drank coffee. Today he handed her an icy gin-and-tonic.

'Don't hold with gin meself,' he remarked. 'But it's what you drink, isn't it?'

She nodded, surprised and pleased, even in the midst of the anxiety that was beginning to infiltrate right through to her bones, that he'd noticed at all, let alone remembered, what she drank.

It wasn't the first time, and it wouldn't be the last, that Leo had to break the hard news to a patient. But this, to his astonishment, was different from all the other occasions. It wasn't, either, that he hadn't been so much involved before. Leo often loved his patients – he'd loved Miss Kilpatrick, for instance. Many others, too.

But as Judith, with her slight young body, her slight and damaged body, sat there opposite him, tautly bracing herself to listen unflinchingly, the pale oval of her face almost as disciplined as Rob's would have been, something happened to Leo. Round him his familiar flat changed its atmosphere and took on a radiance it had never known before.

Correction. It had held this radiance for him once

before. Way back in the past, when all the furniture was new and shining, when he'd been a recently appointed consultant, possessive and delighted with his success. Jane Drummond had come into the flat one day, had sat on his new leather settee, and suffused the room with a glow it had never known since.

Until today.

Judith sat there opposite him, he had only grim news for her, but his flat took her to its heart and deep inside himself he knew he'd come home at last. Jane was behind him, lost in the past, and Judith had come to join him.

He took himself in hand. This was surely no more than some passing lunacy. Nothing would come of it. A weird infatuation, it must be, that would possess him for a moment, and then be gone for ever.

Except that it gave no sign of going.

'About your diagnosis.' He sat down with a thump on his black leather chair, and gave her a straight look from his dark eyes. 'As I told you just now, your father feels it won't help you to know all the possibilities ahead. He – '

'But I must know.' The words exploded across the room.

'He's of the opinion' – Leo sounded his most detached and academic, almost as if he was on a teaching round – 'that as you may never have a recurrence it won't profit you to be made aware of possibilities which very likely will never concern you.'

'I can deal with the worst, once I know it.' The grey eyes were blazing across the room. 'I – I'm quite – well, quite brave' – she sounded almost apologetic about it – 'about facing up to anything. It's the unknown that upsets me, makes me paint disastrous pictures in my mind. Not to mention leaving me unable to make any plans. So tell me. Just tell me straight and leave me to face the consequences. Give, Leo, please.' Her eyes met his, not blazing now, but with that poignant trust in him that seemed to turn his bones to water.

'Multiple sclerosis,' he said baldly. There. It was done. For better or worse.

She stared at him, and then dropped her gaze. Hiding her reaction, he thought painfully.

'Only what I suspected.' She was offhand.

He longed to be able to take her into his arms and comfort her. Only what comfort could he or anyone offer? It was her illness and she had to bear it and live with it for the rest of her days.

She picked up the big ashtray on his coffee table, looked at it unseeingly, turning it round and round in her hands, blindly. 'Incurable,' she stated in a detached fashion. 'I could soon be in a wheelchair, drugged, incontinent, useless.'

'Possible. But not very likely. The chances are against it. But that's what your father was afraid of, you see. That you'd jump to some conclusion of that sort. He wanted to spare you that.'

'I like to look things in the face.'

'Me, too,' he agreed. 'No need, however – ' Just in time he stopped, bit back a crude surgical expression. 'No need to settle for the grimmest possible outlook, is there? Give yourself a bit of a chance, eh? You might never have another symptom – that's quite on the cards. Or you might have a similar experience to the one you've already had in your leg. In your arm, say, like pins and needles again, only it wouldn't go away – but even that might well not happen for twenty or thirty years. All right, once it happens it is incurable.

Or we don't know the cure yet – again, in twenty years we probably will. So no need to get all steamed up. You might easily have perfectly good health until you're abour fifty.'

'Fifty?' She grinned broadly. 'It does seem a good way off, and hardly worth losing sleep over. All the same, tell me truthfully. What do you think is the most likely, that or a wheelchair in the next few years?'

'I'd say you've a seventy-five per cent chance of getting right away with it.' He couldn't put it higher than that.

'And if I don't, if I'm there in a wheelchair inside five years?'

He was harsh. 'Then you must set to and cultivate your mind instead of your body, as many courageous patients have succeeded in doing before you.' This was not the moment for softness. Rather, he had somehow to put her on her mettle, make her take up the fight.

She sat there on the sofa, her expression cool and remote. 'Right,' she said, her voice brittle. 'Thank you for being honest with me. I know now where I stand.'

'Sorry it's been such lousy hearing.'

She shook her tawny head. 'I needed to know. I shall grow accustomed to the idea. Thanks, too, for not treating me like a child.'

'I don't think of you as a child.' And that was true enough. His body was making urgent suggestions about her that had nothing to do with childhood.

'I'm twenty-one,' she said, unaware. 'I've done nearly three years of physiotherapy. I've two parents who are doctors and who talk about very little else, and I've typed my father's case notes since I was in my teens. This must seem nothing to you, but in fact I'm perfectly capable of reading the textbooks myself, and adding up my chances. I just needed to be able to talk

my prognosis over honestly with someone. That's
what they none of them seemed to understand.
Professor Collingham and my father – my mother, too,
when she writes – they all behave as if I'm under age
and in need of care and protection.'

She was right, Leo knew. She was an adult, ready
for an adult's responsibilities, and must be treated as
such, not cosseted as a child. All the same, he wished
he could do a bit of that cosseting himself. To cherish
Judith, to hold her in his arms and look after her for
ever would be the most satisfying and rewarding
experience life could ever hold. While to make love to
her – he pulled himself up sharply. This wouldn't do.
She was ill, a patient, and Rob's only daughter. Her
body was not for him.

He'd take her out to a restaurant – he couldn't risk
remaining alone with her any longer in his flat. There
were limits to self-control.

'Let's go out and have a bite,' he suggested hastily.

'Eat, drink and be merry,' she said, her mouth
quirking.

'For tomorrow we die, you mean? Nuts. I'm just
hungry.'

He took her to Rule's, one of his favourite
restaurants, fed her on roast beef and gave her a
mellow Burgundy to drink. 'Do no harm to feed you
up a bit.'

She smiled her amazing amile, but he saw sadly
that her thoughts were not with him at all. He
understood the reason. She hadn't yet talked herself
out. She wasn't ready for light-hearted chat about
nothing. What she needed was to chew over her
illness.

'The only way to cope with a setback like yours,' he
remarked, 'is to force yourself to treat it as an

opportunity. All right, so you've got a problem. You can't after all do exactly as you'd planned. But in this life you have to be resilient. Ready at any stage to pick yourself up and start again. Your body may be letting you down, but there's nothing wrong with your mind, is there? So develop it. In a way you might not have had time for while your affairs were running along smoothly in the right direction. What sort of person are you inside? Not just your father's daughter, or your mother's, either. You're an individual.'

She was startled. 'You've put it into words. Exactly what I've been feeling. I've sort of had to come up against myself, hard, and I'm beginning to wonder if I'm at all the kind of person I thought I was.' She cut up roast beef, pondering, and then began talking about her parents. She'd always, she explained, admired her father and tried to be like him. 'A good reliable doctor, a kind man – he is, you know, however controlled and distant he seems. He's a complete contrast to my mother.' She shook her head. 'I used to think they made a well-balanced pair. Because she's affectionate and outgoing, very easy to get on with compared with Dad. She's bossy, it's true, but that's just her way. I used to be so proud of the fact that she was a cardiologist on Northiam's unit – yet now there's a side of me that can't forgive her for clearing off to the States with him when he went, instead of staying here with Dad and me. Dad doesn't blame her. He says she had to do it. But I – well, I can't help feeling she ought to have thought twice, and I have tried, ever since she left, to make up to Dad for being on his own. Even to me the flat was so empty, after she'd gone, and what it must have been like for Dad I daren't think.'

'All this is about your parents.'

She looked surprised. 'I suppose so.'

'What about *you*?'

She shook her head, her tawny head that he longed to cradle. 'I suppose I simply don't know,' she admitted. 'I'm an unknown quantity to me, that's what I've been discovering. I seem to be just a person who reacts to others. I don't know what I am myself. Except I like working for you.' She gave him the brilliance of her transfiguring smile.

His body responded instantly, but like a Victorian gentleman he pushed firmly aside what would then have been called his baser instincts (though he would have chosen quite another label). 'I'm glad,' he said mildly. How glad, she could have no notion – and just as well. 'But why? Bit of a comedown, I should have thought it must seem.'

'I thought it would be.' As usual, she made no attempt to gloss over the unflattering truth. 'I only took it on because Sophie nagged, and I thought it would be a good plan to get out of the flat, stop mooning about feeling sorry for myself. But I love it. The activity and all the people – you and the surgeons, the ward staff and the patients, and the people in Harley Street, too. And I like being responsible for – for producing the paperwork that results in patients coming in for surgery and then going home again. The job has a purpose.'

'Oh, it has that all right.'

'And it isn't all office work, either. I don't just stay put at a typewriter and a telephone, as I'd imagined secretaries did. There's driving you, and being sometimes in Harley Street and sometimes at the hospital. Ward rounds. Chasing things up – you know, down to radiology or over to records, up to the theatre to find you, or over to outpatients. It's all fun.

That's what's a bit shattering, and quite unlike training to be a physio, which always seemed – well, demanding, but terribly earnest. Or that's how I found it. I'm beginning to wonder if I was cut out for it at all.'

'What made you go into it? You must have had a reason.'

She shrugged her narrow shoulders. 'It was a second choice, I'm afraid. I'd wanted to do medicine. But it's such long training, and the chances of getting in are even slimmer now than when my parents began. And Dad was against it. A hard grind, he said, and especially for a woman. Look at my mother, he pointed out, how she's had to choose between her job and her family. I'd have to make the same choice, according to him. It sounds a bit old-world, but he's right, isn't he? Look at us – my parents and me. I didn't want that all over again. No, thanks. Not ever. And I thought as a physio it'd be easy to have a job and some home life.'

'Strikes me you may have been too close to your parents and what seems to have gone wrong for them to be able to make a true choice.'

'Yes, you're right. My decision was all muddled up. I suppose, looking back, I can see that part of it was based on a sort of competitiveness with my mother. It's not that I'm not awfully fond of her, but I have been a bit fanatical about managing to avoid her problems.'

'I can see how that would happen. It was a good deal simpler for me – unlike you, I came from right outside the hospital world.' For the first time in years, he wanted to relate the story of his boyhood and his family background, all so untypical for a consultant at the Central, to this one attentive listener who, he was beginning to fear, he loved to the point of madness.

When he'd started his student years, he remembered, he'd felt – and been – an oddity. People had made jokes about him. About his appearance – he'd been much fatter then – his behaviour, his vocabulary.

Those days were over, though. Finished. He'd made good, although it had been harder for him than most of them. 'I was the first one from my family to train as a doctor,' was all he allowed himself to say to Judith. 'I did it because I had to. I didn't know why, no one told me it was a good idea, nothing like that. I just knew it was what I was going to do, and I went off and did it, regardless.

She listened, her grey eyes alive with sympathy. What Leo had not permitted himself to say was already known to her. Rob Chasemore had been a registrar when Leo had first hit the Central as a student, and he'd told his daughter about the impact the greengrocer's boy had made. It all seemed a far cry from the bulky, expensively suited, confident surgeon sitting opposite her now, and even further from the consultant she worked for in Harley Street and around the hospital. But wherever they happened to be, his presence excited her, and her own future, which should have been dark and worrying, instead gleamed invitingly ahead. When he deposited her back at her father's flat she was alive with an inexplicable sense of anticipation, and though she sat down at the desk in her room to think over seriously what he'd said about remaking her life, treating her illness and the change of direction it entailed as an opportunity, she found her thoughts insisted on dwelling, not on herself but on her new chief.

The next day, in Harley Street, he suddenly asked her about her daily régime.

'Used to be athletic, right?'

'Well, yes, I suppose so. In a way.' Athletic was not at all a word she would have chosen, nor was she in any way delighted to hear him use it to describe her, calling up as it did some beefy hockey-playing Amazon.

'Can't play games at present. So what sort of exercise and fresh air are you getting?'

This was too much. Leo was notorious for getting neither himself, ever. 'Honestly,' she retorted. 'How you can talk. Tell me what you get in the way of fresh air and exercise?'

He grinned at her. 'Not a question of do what I do,' he said. 'Do what I say. Anyway you're wrong. Do take exercise.'

'You *do*? But – '

'Just don't 'appen to care for making an exhibition of meself.'

'So where – and when?' She eyed him quizzically.

The look had an immediate effect on him, and he longed, like a boastful boy, to be able to announce triumphs hidden from the Central to astonish her. He fought this, with other more demanding urges, down, and remarked only 'the cardiologists were always nagging me, so a few years back I gave into them and bought meself an exercise bike. It's in me study. Use it daily, I do. You can 'ave a pedal on it, if you want.'

'Oh, I would like to. Thank you very much.' Crazily, she was perhaps more excited at the opportunity he was giving her to wander round his flat more or less as she chose than at his interest in her régime. From the beginning she'd been fascinated by

Leo's flat – so unlike her own home, furnished by Daphne and Rob with good pieces of furniture as they were able to afford them, and hung with hard-wearing neutral wallpaper and brocade curtains of a pronounced lack of originality. Leo's flat, in contrast, had colour, sparkle and lavish comfort, and she'd been hoping for weeks now that, with Sophie's job, she might also inherit the freedom of Leo's home.

'Swimming?' he was asking her. 'Do any swimming, ever?' This, though she never guessed it, was courtship.

She shook her head. 'Not these days. It's silly, I know, but I feel so embarrassed when I use the hospital pool. So many of the physios there are friends of mine, and I hate being there as a patient, so that they feel they have to come over and see how I'm doing, and hang around making conversation while they watch my every movement to see if I'm unco-ordinated and deteriorating. So I haven't been for ages. And I don't much want to.' Pink in the face, she glared rebelliously at him, while her final words came pouring out in an obstinate rush.

His heart bled for her, but he merely patted her hand reassuringly. 'Don't panic, love. You don't have to. I'll take you along to a nice little pool, not a physio or a medical practitioner in sight. Apart from meself, that is. Are you on?'

'I'm on,' she told him, relaxed and easy again.

'Right, we'll fix it.' He had to drag his own eyes away from hers. He had a new hobby. Judith-watching. However, riffling through the pages of his diary, he gave no sign of any interest other than a preoccupation with dates and times, and Judith had no inkling he was doing more than involving himself in her progress as routinely as he would have done with any convalescent patient or member of his staff. Finally he shook his head. 'Got no gaps, nowhere. Not for weeks.'

Disappointment flooded her. She set her lips. 'Never mind.' She was curt, dismissive. 'It doesn't matter at all.'

'Does matter. We're gonna go swimming. Look, are you any good at early rising?'

'How early?'

She was as cautious as Rob, he thought. However, the ways in which she didn't resemble her father were what interested him. Involuntarily, he grinned at the thought, and remarked cheerfully 'I was thinking we might swim before breakfast. How'd that be?'

'Swim before breakfast? What fun.' Her mouth curved entrancingly, and the grey eyes came alight again.

'Pick you up then, at the main entrance of y'r block, shall I? Say at seven-thirty.'

'I'll be there.'

'We can have a quick swim and a cup of coffee.'

'Great.' She was radiant now, and he wanted to hug her.

His body approved of this proposal, suggesting, too, that hugging need by no means be the end of the story, either.

Well, what the hell. Why should it be?

At this juncture his ever-ready chaperon, the telephone, butted in. Judith, who after all was his secretary – and they did happen to be in his office, too – promptly answered it, and the moment was gone.

Two days later, though, he picked her up in the Mercedes, drove through a few side-roads, parked, and walked into an austere-looking building off Gray's Inn Road.

'Municipal baths,' he informed her, paying the entrance fee and setting off purposefully along a drab corridor. 'Bin coming here ever since I was a kid.'

They had the pool almost to themselves, apart from a few serious swimmers methodically doing some self-appointed daily number of lengths. Leo, in maroon trunks, dived surprisingly neatly in, and did a couple of lengths himself, before coming to join her, a slim, elegant girl in a black swimsuit and cap, floating on her back and splashing her legs dutifully. 'You look like a seal,' he told her. 'Race you to the end and back.'

Afterwards he took her to breakfast in his flat. 'I'll have to go in, to see if there are any messages, so we might as well eat there. OK?'

He'd planned this with some care, but nothing of the sort occurred to Judith, who said only 'Yes, of course,' in a brisk little voice that effectively disguised the delight she was feeling.

They sat on high bar-stools at the tiled counter in his streamlined kitchen, eating scrambled eggs, drinking a strong and fragrant brew of coffee produced by his machine, and talking their way methodically through his appointments.

She could take the Mercedes on to Harley Street, he said, dropping him off at the hospital on the way. She could call back for him after his ward round – he'd ring her when he was ready. He'd sign his letters, then they could snatch a sandwich somewhere for lunch and afterwards, since it was his afternoon for seeing patients in Harley Street, he'd go back there with her.

The day followed this appointed course and, to end it, he took her out to a meal. Finally, dropping her off at the Chasemores' flat on his way to the hospital to see a patient, he remarked, 'Got me list tomorrow morning. So shan't be able to swim. How about the day after, though? Like another pre-breakfast dip?'

'I'd love it.'

'I'll pick you up again, then. Seven-thirty. Here. Day after tomorrow.'

'Lovely. Thank you, Leo.'

He drove off to the Central and the patient who was worrying him, while Judith, bemused, let herself into the flat and thought about her day. She had spent most of it with Leo, and it had been heaven. Would they, could they possibly, go on like this?

They could. They did. Their days together began to assume a pattern, beginning with the morning swim, continuing with breakfast in Leo's flat, and going on with interruptions to the evening, when, somewhere or other, they'd usually have supper together, though not necessarily alone. Often, in fact, Judith, although with Leo, was no more than one in a crowd. In the hospital, no one took much notice of the amount of time they spent together. They were used to Sophie's presence in Leo's life, and took Judith equally for granted as her replacement.

Leo, though, was constantly asking himself what he supposed he was up to. It was not possible, surely, that he had fallen head over heels in love, at his age, and with Rob Chasemore's daughter, of all people?

After all these years and all these girlfriends, surely he wasn't proposing to end up with someone who was probably going to be in precarious health all her life, suffering from a chronic and incurable condition?

So what about turning his attention back to the beautiful Stella? She'd proved to be an excellent theatre sister, quick, deft and with excellent anticipation. She continued to cast him speaking glances from those languorous brown eyes above her

mask, and if he gave his mind to it, he was fairly sure
she'd be his for the taking. She'd soon forget that
damned Larry of hers, leave him behind in the past, if
Leo showed he was interested in her. But he had no
desire to take her into his bed.

He wanted to make love to Judith. His body
hungered for her, and seldom stopped reminding him
of the fact.

But here he had forced himself to place an embargo.
He couldn't make love to Judith Chasemore. Even if
she'd been in perfect health, to have an affair with her
would have been awkward. And as matters were, with
Judith acting as his secretary entirely because of the
doubtful state of her health, the arrangement talked
over in detail beforehand with her father, no one but a
lecherous maniac would try to seduce the girl. No,
with Judith it would have to be marriage or nothing.

Forget it. She was a good secretary – much better,
in fact, than he'd dared hope. So he might as well
settle for reality, be thankful that Judith was shaping
up well as a substitute for Sophie, and be satisfied.

Satisfied? He wanted a quite different sort of
satisfaction.

For years, he reminded himself irritably, he'd been
fond of Sophie. He'd depended on her, they'd got on
well, and she'd become like a young sister. So why
couldn't that infuriating Judith Chasemore turn into
another young sister?

The arguments raged in his mind and body, but the
answer always came out the same. He wanted to make
love to Judith.

He found himself behaving like an infatuated boy.
He'd ring through to Harley Street, asking an
unnecessary question, simply to hear her voice. He'd
call in to see if there were any queries, or a letter to

sign, only because he was unable to keep away. He began to demand her presence at his side not only on his teaching round, which was customary, but at an increasing number of routine assignments where he'd previously been ready to dictate notes on to his machine.

He seemed, as well, to have become a keen swimmer. Breakfast after swimming with Judith in his flat, planning the day together – it had become like a drug. He couldn't do without it.

Judith Chasemore, he had to face it, so like Rob – except when she was entirely herself suddenly and not even faintly reminiscent of her father – with her hesitant walk, her slender body and her hair like autumn leaves, Judith had captured his heart. She was argumentative and could be difficult, she was apt to take offence if treated too much like any sort of invalid. He wanted to take care of her for the rest of her days.

# Chapter 6

Just as well, Leo decided, that he was leaving for his
lecture tour in the USA at the beginning of August.
This freakish infatuation would undoubtedly have
vanished when he returned, and he'd be able to lead a
normal life again.

He could see Melanie, too, in New York. That
would bring him to his senses.

Sophie came down to the office and fixed his travel,
though she did it with Judith alongside her, she
explained. Next year, Judith would be ready to handle
all the arrangements herself.

For some reason this picture upset him, though he
couldn't have said why. He frowned, and Sophie, at
once assuming that he was doubting Judith's
efficiency, began to defend her.

From bad to worse. What was happening to him,
that he could no longer have a straight talk with
Sophie? He sighed, and fixed his attention sternly on
travel details.

He was crossing the Atlantic in company with
James Leyburn and his wife Emily. James was the
assistant director of the Central's cardiothoracic
department, and was going to California to spend a
month with his former chief, Marcus Northiam, now
Director of Heart Surgery at the Ocean Hospital. Leo
himself had an invitation from Northiam to spend a
week at the end of his tour to unwind in the

Californian sun and swim in the Pacific. Apart from
the well-known fact that to relax and unwind
anywhere in the vicinity of Northiam was impossible –
one of the world's busiest heart surgeons, his
departure for the USA had rocked the Central – the
programme appealed.

Leo's lecture tour whirled by at a furious pace. He
lectured, he talked, he went on ward rounds, he was
invited to slip in extra sessions of demonstrating or
watching surgery in far-flung hospitals – to which
American surgeons drove him, after huge American
hospitality, in large, fast cars. Then they gave him
more hospitality, drove him to the airport, he flew to
another city, and the cycle repeated itself. It was
exhilarating.

Or it ought to have been exhilarating. It always had
been in the past. When he'd been on one of these tours
before, he'd been stimulated and refreshed, however
tired he was, and had returned to the Central spilling
over with vitality and new ideas. This year he found it
not only tiring, but worse than that, increasingly
tiresome. An interruption of his real life. They were
such nice people. Interesting, too. But he wanted none
of them. He wanted simply to be back home with
Judith.

He must be getting old.

Again the flicker of anxiety. Could he possibly be
going to repeat his father's pattern? Burnt out in his
forties, finished? Within a few more years, his life over
and done with? Was the drive to the top – which,
however strenuous, had always been fun – over?

Judith would bring comfort. If he could talk to her
about these ridiculous feelings, everything would be
all right. But not so much as a letter came from her.
He'd watched out for his mail as eagerly as an eight-

year-old in Christmas week. But to his acute disappointment his weekly letter from the home front, in the past arriving regularly from Sophie, continued to be sent by her. And Nick, running both his department and his private practice in his absence, added his own notes to Sophie's letters. The theatre was closed for its annual cleaning, as many of the staff as possible were taking their holidays — August was always a quiet month for patients — and the department was peaceful. It was sensible of Sophie and Nick to send him what amounted to a joint report on the few remaining in-patients, the emergency admissions, a few routine discharges and a few unexpected ones. It was a good plan. But he tore the envelopes apart, searching for an enclosure from Judith, and scanned the pages of Sophie's letters hunting for a reference to Judith.

Perhaps she'd gone on holiday, too.

Without telling him? He was unpleasantly jolted. He was being even more ridiculous, he reminded himself fiercely. Rob Chasemore might well have taken a break, gone off somewhere with his daughter. Leo found that the possibility that he couldn't even picture Judith in his mind's eye, as he'd been doing, going daily from the Chasemores' flat to his own big room in Harley Street, upset him. He felt lost. He shook his head angrily. If anyone else had told him of feelings like this, he'd have laughed his head off. He'd have assumed, too, that they'd quickly come to their senses and understand how lunatic they'd been.

The lecture tour continued on its frenetic course. Invitations continued to shower on him from all sides, but he managed, in spite of himself, to find time to go on thinking about Judith. Worrying about her — where the hell was she? Longing for her.

What he failed to find time for was a visit to Melanie in New York. Almost every evening he told himself he was going to ring her, but he never did. He hadn't rung her when he passed through New York at the start of his programme, and he didn't ring her now from Detroit at the conclusion of it. He could easily have cancelled his week at the Ocean Hospital – which had in any case dwindled to four days – and spent his last weekend with Melanie. But he discovered he didn't want to do this.

It would be good to be back at the Central.

Only another few days – with old friends, too. He'd tell Northiam he was opting out of work and new meetings, taking a few days' rest, as he'd originally suggested.

Unusual for him to adopt this attitude, of course, and both Northiam and Leyburn were surprised. Northiam, who was engrossed, as usual, in his department, hardly noticed. But James Leyburn was perturbed.

'Leo, you look whacked. Are you all right?'

'Do feel a bit tired, must admit. Odd. This tour seems to have taken it out of me more than usual – normally I thrive on the 'ole shemozzle. Must be getting old.' This had become his constant fear. Old. He was getting old and tired. Too old for Judith. How much younger was she, anyway? Fifteen years? Or more? He sighed heavily.

James Leyburn watched him with a good deal of anxiety. 'I prescribe complete dropping out for the next three days, at any rate. Swim and laze about. You're still carrying far too much weight around with you, you know. It doesn't help. No good can come of it. Seriously, Leo, you ought to consider making a real attempt to lose some of it.'

Leo nodded. 'So I'm constantly telling meself. But it's not so easy. Got a big appetite, I have, and need me strength, too. In the operating theatre, I mean, not what you're imagining, you coarse fellow. Honest, mate, it's a problem. Mrs Noakes runs mostly to trad.'

'Yes, I see there's a difficulty there.' At the Central they knew that Leo had solved his domestic needs years back by taking on the wife of the head porter. She cooked both for her own family and for him in her own home, dumped the results in his refrigerator or freezer with written instructions on reheating attached, and fitted in his housework with her own at hours to suit herself. The arrangement had worked splendidly for years, but no one would have described Mrs Noakes as an imaginative cook.

At Heathrow, in spite of himself, Leo peered about hopefully for Judith. Far from losing his madness in the States, recovering from what he had once, aeons back, imagined to be mere infatuation, he was more in love with her than ever. She'd been with him in spirit throughout his lecture tour. He'd attempted to turn his back on her again and again, but at any odd moment, sometimes not even when he was alone, the most ordinary sights or the simplest phrases could unexpectedly bring her to disturbing life.

And now he had to turn his back on his longing for her yet again. For there was Sophie, his darling blonde Soph, very large and pregnant, come loyally to meet him and the Leyburns in the Mercedes. He hugged her as enthusiastically as always, the Leyburns greeted her, and they set off for Harley Street, where Sophie informed them she had dinner waiting.

'Dinner? Is that the time?' He was amazed. In that case, he thought miserably, no chance that he'd find Judith in his office, as he'd been hoping. He kept his disappointment to himself, and throughout the delicious – but strictly non-fattening – meal Sophie gave them, he and the Leyburns told tales of their travels and the Ocean Hospital – James had some new and hilarious stories to relate about Marcus Northiam, as brusque and egotistic as ever, his heart surgery, though, as brilliant as it had always been.

'I'm glad he's safely in California,' James admitted. 'Because I really couldn't stand large doses of him any longer. But he's quite outstanding, and it was a privilege to work with him again for a few short weeks.'

'All right, so it was a privilege,' Emily interposed. 'But if you'd seen him steaming back to our room each night, the air blue with his curses.'

James grinned. 'In short,' he said, 'I'm glad to be back. Working with Tom Rennison will be like joining an old friend again.'

Almost immediately after the meal, he and Emily departed to join the Rennisons and hear the lowdown on what had been happening in the cardiothoracic department in their absence. Leo would have liked to have left with them, but as soon as they made a move, Nick left Sophie to see them out, and began, in his turn, bringing Leo up to date with affairs in general surgery, so that it was half an hour later before he was able to enquire, in what he hoped was a suitably casual manner, about Judith.

'Oh, she's been in the private wing, with Professor Collingham putting her through it,' Sophie told him.

His heart dropped. 'The private wing? What for? Not had another episode, has she?' Unusually for him, he was panicking.

'No, nothing like that.' Sophie was as placid as a plate of rice pudding, and for once Leo could have shaken her. 'She's out now, back at home, in any case. She only went in for observation, a load of tests, and so on. I didn't tell you about it in my letters, because she asked me not to. She said she'd rather be back in the office before I told you – I think she thought you'd have worried about the office work.'

'No, I shouldn't. Know perfectly well you can handle it – what does the silly girl think? Haven't you been looking after it for years? Why didn't she tell me what she was up to?'

Sophie was easy. 'Anyway, she came round yesterday to clue herself in, and she came in again this morning and more or less took over. When you're back on Thursday she'll be running things in the ordinary way.'

'Should have told me.' Leo was obviously put out, but Sophie, although she could see he was thrown, imagined this to be the result of jet-lag and fatigue. Accordingly, when he suggested going, she almost pushed him out of the front door to return, she supposed, to his own flat and catch up on his sleep.

'Mrs Noakes has left everything ready for you,' she said, before she shut the door on him.

Leo, in spite of his exhaustion, made for the Chasemores' flat at a good pace. Judith, wearing the familiar jeans and one of her striped T-shirts, opened the door to him herself, looking, he was astonished and relieved to find, exactly the same as when he had left. She hadn't changed one iota during his absence. She was the Judith he'd been dreaming about all these weeks – if not more so.

'How are you, love?' he asked tenderly, taking her cosily into his arms.

'Fine,' she said. 'Especially now you're back. I didn't suppose – ' she broke off. A give-away remark had all but escaped her. She'd been about to let him know she'd been counting not merely the days but the hours to his return. Being held by him like this was great, too, though she hastily reminded herself that Leo had always been demonstrative. He'd hug patients, ward sisters, theatre sisters – particularly theatre sisters, she remembered, and her stomach contracted. Leo was in love with Stella. Everyone knew it. He was hugging her, Judith, only because she was his secretary, an unimportant member of his team, and he'd just returned from the States.

'What didn't you suppose?' he asked, though in fact he knew very well. Something had changed during his absence. Now that he was back she seemed to be an open book to him, her every thought apparent. He knew at once that she'd been missing him and looking forward to his return, and he was consumed by a new surging joy. All the same, he wasn't going to let her get away with secretive, inhibited reactions like her father's. Not with him, she wouldn't. 'Cough it up, duckie,' he added, giving her – unaccountably she was reposing still within the span of his arms – a small shake.

'That you'd think – or have a chance – of coming round here so soon after you got back,' she said in a small voice that rapidly, under the influence of being held so sturdily, gained strength and finished quite strongly. 'But am I glad you did.' Her face was alight in the fashion he was never able to forget. 'Oh, it's great to see you.'

'It's great to see you, too.' Relinquishing his grasp with one arm, he kept the other round her shoulders and walked her through to the Chasemore's sitting-room. 'What's all this about you having to be admitted to the private wing?'

He'd come round only because of her health. Not because of her as a person at all. Simply because she was on his staff, and he always looked after anyone on his staff. Sophie or Nick must have told him she'd been admitted. 'I'm perfectly all right,' she said crisply, and twitched herself out of his enfolding arm.

Luckily for her, he was still reading her clearly. He grinned, reclaimed her, and said amiably, 'Come and sit down here and tell me all about it.' He pushed her down on to the sofa, established himself at her side, put his arm back round her slight and angry shoulders, and took her hand into his. 'Shoot, love. What's bin on the go while I've bin out of the country?'

She knew he would have been just the same with a patient. With Miss Kilpatrick, for instance. Even so, sitting beside him like this was extraordinarily reassuring, and suddenly she was after all ready to unburden herself. 'It was just that once you'd left I had time to think everthing out, and I decided I ought to see Professor Collingham again, now I knew my own diagnosis, and talk it all out properly with him. So I did, and he was really quite easy to talk to. Anyway, we both came to the conclusion it would be a good idea if I had some more tests, and so on, and he said I'd better go in and have them, so I'd be available. I'd far rather have stayed here and gone in each day, but he was adamant, and Dad backed him up, so I didn't see how to get out of it. If you hadn't been away – ' she broke off, not sure what she meant.

Leo had no doubt. 'I'd have put a stop to it, seen you stayed at home. That's right.' He was pleased at the picture called up, and delighted to find there was no hideous meaning behind her spell in the private wing. He grinned at her, his dark eyes alive with

humour and, she saw without a shade of doubt, with
something else, too.

She began at last, in her turn, to read him clearly.
'Oh, Leo,' she told him, 'I have missed you.
Everything's quite different when you're away.'

'It is?' He not only lit up instantaneously like a
Christmas tree but expanded visibly, seemed twice as
large. He felt twice as large, too. Experimentally he
kissed her.

She kissed him back.

After what seemed to both of them a lifetime, they
tilted their heads back and looked at one another,
wide eyed.

'Bin wanting to do that for a long time,' he said. All
the doubts and hesitations were past. He was going to
make love to this girl. He was going to take her into his
bed and make passionate love to her for hours and
hours. Days and days. Weeks. Months. For ever. He
was going to marry her and have children by her, start
a family.

'What's the time?' he asked abruptly.

She was startled. After all that, had he another
appointment? Crestfallen, she consulted her watch,
and told him.

'Good God, is it really? Feels like breakfast-time – I
was thinking we had the day ahead of us – though I
ought to have known better, Soph gave me a huge
meal and said it was dinner.'

'How long have you been up?'

He rubbed his eyes. 'No idea. I've altered me
watch.' He was thinking that although the last thing
he wanted was another large meal, he ought to take
her out to dinner. Afterwards, they could go back to
his flat. But he couldn't simply rise to his feet now and
say, 'Over to my flat and into bed'. Even he, even with

this dream of a girl he'd discovered, couldn't quite do that.

Why not?

To his rage, the reason why not proved to be Rob, who walked into his own flat at precisely the wrong moment, and proceeded to interrogate Leo about his trip, first of all, and then went on to bring him meticulously up to date on every patient who'd been through intensive care during his absence.

'Shall I make some coffee?' Judith asked. 'Or tea?'

'Cup of tea 'ud be great,' Leo said.

Never, he thought, had he seen anyone pour tea more gracefully. He watched Judith's fingers curl themselves round the handle of the big silver pot — trust the Chasemores to possess such an object — then her arm lift while elbow and wrist formed an arc of beauty as the amber stream splashed into eggshell china cups — so different from the pottery mug in which Sophie gave him his tea. What would he feel, though, if Judith's illness affected not only her right foot, but crept insidiously through her body as the nerve sheaths came under its grip, and the gesture of pouring tea became first clumsy and finally impossible? How would he react to the daily drag of an invalid wife, unable to look after herself, let alone manage his home?

If this were Judith he'd be proud, glad, thankful to be able to do anything at all to help her.

While his thoughts wandered, his eyes devoured her, and his body throbbed its unmistakable message of desire. Meanwhile Rob, having completed his rundown of patients, embarked on a long discussion about post-operative care, until at last, presumably noticing that Leo's mind was not entirely on what he was saying, he packed him off home to his own flat, reminding him about jet-lag and talking robustly of a good night's sleep. By now, to his fury, Leo had to admit that he was more or less out for the count.

'I'll see him out.' Judith was quick.

Rob, glad, if the truth had been known, to see his daughter displaying a proper hostess-like attitude to his colleague and her own chief, sank back into his chair, saying only 'Night, then. See you in the department – day after tomorrow, is it?'

'That's right.' Leo followed Judith out to the spacious hall, and took her back into his arms. 'Tomorrow?' he suggested finally. 'I've the day free – we'll go out somewhere, how would that be?'

'Fantastic.'

# Chapter 7

Leo woke knowing it was going to be a wonderful day. He reached for the telephone, and rang the Chasemore flat.

Rob answered, correct and businesslike as ever. 'Chasemore.'

'Hi, Rob. Leo here. Can I 'ave a word with Jude?'

Rob, assuming Leo was going to tell his daughter to collect some tapes for typing, or ask her to perform some similar chore, thought nothing of this. 'Sure,' he said. 'Hold on.'

Judith came on the line. 'Leo?'

'Hiya. Care for a swim?'

'Love one.'

'Pick you up in fifteen minutes.' He put the telephone down.

Judith rushed back to her room, pulled off the old jeans she was wearing, and dragged on a ludicrously expensive velour tracksuit she'd acquired with Leo in mind. All his lovely ladies, so fashionable and sophisticated – she knew no way of competing with them. While he'd been in the States, though, she'd done something else besides talking to Professor Collingham and having her tests. She'd done a despairing round of the big stores, and trodden gingerly into a few unnerving boutiques. She'd been out of her element, and she'd had the sense to recognise it. Her one moment of madness had been to buy a dreamy caftan from Morocco, white silk heavily embroidered with gold thread and pearly beads, in which, though she could see she looked quite ravishing, she knew she'd never dare appear in public. After that, she'd returned to the type of garment she understood, and chosen extravagantly from the sports outfitter she'd used for years. The tracksuit, a vivid green, did things for her figure and her hair and somehow managed to be both concealing and suggestive. The sales girl had been ecstatic, and had insisted that what she needed to complete the outfit was a pair of zippy ankle boots and a matching sling bag. The look was very much of the moment. A year earlier or a year later it would have seemed odd and peculiar, but just for today it was a riveting success, and as Judith peered at herself in her bedroom mirror she knew it. Oozing confidence from every pore and beaming widely like an expectant child, as Leo drew up in the Mercedes she stepped out of the entrance to the block of flats.

'Pow!' He stared at her. 'Wot a treat. 'Op in, love. We're going places.'

All day they went places, and everywhere was magic.

They swam together in the pool, and he put his strong hands on her slight waist. She was the most beautiful creature he'd ever held, he told her. She was well aware that there was no possibility this could be true, but to hear him say it was bliss.

They returned together to his flat to breakfast, and looked out on to a panorama of roofs glinting in the morning sun. For the weather was with them. It was going to be a perfect day.

He asked her how she'd like to spend it.

Provided she was with him, she didn't, in fact, care. 'Anyhow.'

He nearly took her straight to bed, but Rob the previous evening in the flat, and then again this morning on the telephone, had reactivated his scruples.

'Town or country?' he asked.

'Country would be heaven. I hardly ever see it.' Living all her days in the shadow of the hospital, attending a nearby day school, Judith was totally a Londoner and knew almost nothing of the countryside. The Chasemores had no weekend cottage, their holidays had usually been spent travelling, and since Daphne had moved to California, mainly in America or Canada.

'Not much of a country-goer, meself,' Leo said.

Her heart sank. He'd wanted to spend the day in town. She ought to have remembered. Around the hospital everyone said Leo was not an outdoor man at all, but a sophisticated city-dweller.

Everyone said a good deal about Leo. No one but she knew he came swimming before breakfast.

No one? Presumably Melanie knew.

She had to forget Melanie and hold on to today. Live for the moment. The wonderful, unutterably lovely now.

'Never 'ave seen the point of driving miles to glimpse the sea,' he was saying. 'Or stand on some blooming 'ill to be blown apart by an arctic wind in order to say I've seen seven counties. But what I do know is London's country. Like the Green Line coach brochures say. Care to explore London's country with me, or rather go further afield?'

She would have gone anywhere with him.

'Richmond Park,' he said. 'Know it?'

'We've been through it once or twice on the way to Hampton Court, I think.'

'Dare say. I'll show it to you proper.'

Relaxed bodily after the swim – though inwardly churning with wild excitement – Judith sprawled catlike across the orange leather upholstery of the big car while he drove her out of London. He knew every inch of the city, it seemed, cutting through side-streets, making no errors over one-way systems, and within twenty minutes they entered the gates of Richmond Park. 'This is it,' he told her. He was proprietorial, and pointed out views of the park, of the Surrey hills, and of the London they'd left behind as if he owned the entire landscape, every acre of it. 'Move a bit further round, and you'll be able to see the Tower of London.' Enthusiasm spurted exuberantly from him.

Judith wasn't particularly interested in the park or the view. Only in Leo. This car, with him beside her, was her world. And it was more than enough. Happiness was no more than being driven by Leo for ever. Anywhere. Nowhere. In circles round and round the hospital. It would have been all the same to her.

He was happy, too. She was being shewn a side of himself he'd never brought out for anyone before. He'd taken a step back into the past where an excited boy had once explored a new country, and he wanted to take her with him, back into a time when all the world had been filled and brimming over with promise.

However, he soon made a brisk return to a more familiar style. 'London looks a lot better in the distance than it does close to,' he commented. 'Dare say you've seen enough.' Slow he had never been, and he picked up her disinterest in what he'd been showing her almost before she was aware of it herself. He must have been boring her.

He drove smartly out of the park, earlier than he'd intended. 'We'll stop a bit here. Richmond Hill, this is. We can have a drink and a meal, and then I'll take you shopping in the town.' He led the way into a restaurant on the hill, and the excited boy vanished without a trace. He was the old familiar Leo, ordering drinks, choosing a lavish lunch. They sat at a table in the window, so that below them the Thames wound its way towards Windsor, while in the distance the Surrey hills rose in a blue and misty blur. He ignored this view, and watched Judith. 'When we've eaten,' he told her, 'we'll go down into Richmond and buy something for you, to go with that snazzy green outfit. Emeralds are what it needs, of course.'

Judith laughed immoderately.

'Yes, well, dare say that might be goin' a bit far.' Too far, too fast, too soon, he thought with resignation. The idea of buying her at least one emerald pleased him enormously. But it wouldn't do, he could see that. She'd merely be horrified and embarrassed, and the day would be ruined. 'Buy some green beads, eh?' he suggested hopefully. 'To set off y'r suit. And a bangle, say.' He liked the notion of that graceful wrist of Judith's wearing a bracelet of his, showing it off. Showing off her own grace, more likely.

Judith, although she was longing for Leo to buy her some wildly extravagant piece of miraculous jewellery, for her to treasure for ever as a memento of this blissful day, was adamant. No emeralds. No beads. No bracelets. She couldn't let it happen. Her upbringing rose within her, informing her sternly that purchases of jewellery were out.

'We'll drive down and have a wander round,

anyway,' he said. He took her out of the restaurant and back to the Mercedes, drove down Richmond Hill and into the town, succeeded in finding a parking place on the Green, and led her through crowded little alleys stuffed with tiny shops.

'Let's just window shop,' Judith urged. 'Aren't they fun, these shops? The furniture is lovely' – at least that should be safe, he wouldn't try and buy her a chest of drawers, would he? – 'and the china and glass. It's like an exhibition. I'd really rather not think about buying anything, just gaze about me.'

'OK, if that's the way you want it.' He sounded crestfallen as a child.

Unthinkingly she took his arm. 'Leo, you don't mind, do you?' she asked anxiously. 'I'm having such a super time – you don't really want to do any shopping, do you?'

Not with her hanging on his arm like that and looking into his eyes. All ambitions in the shopping line left him abruptly, though until that moment they'd been quite strong. All he wanted now was to take her to bed. He thought of the car, and the flat, and turned back the way they'd come. And then he had a different idea. A new and immensely satisfying plan began to evolve in his imagination.

He remembered the miracle she'd worked in his flat, that day when she'd sat on his chesterfield and the room had swung into radiance round her. He'd take her to his other home, the one he'd secretly been unable to bear since his mother's death. Judith was the one person in the world who could bring it back to life and happiness. He'd let her glimpse it from the river first, see how she reacted to that, and then, perhaps ...

He almost threw her into the car, and drove off out

of Richmond, pulling up about five minutes later, still in a hurry. 'We have to walk from here,' he told her, and set off fast.

Judith followed him cheerfully. It didn't matter to her where she went.

She found herself on the river bank, just by a lock.

Leo forged ahead, and crossed over, via a lock gate, to an island. He gestured upriver. 'Above here,' he informed her, 'the Thames ceases to be a tidal river. Below the lock, it still is.'

Judith was fascinated. 'Tidal? You really mean the tide rises and falls, as if we were at the sea?'

'That's right. It rises and falls in Richmond – I could have shown you. Didn't think of it. Come on, they're going to shut the gates. I always like watching this.'

They leaned together on the railing above the lock, where the water was low, and looked down on to the vessels tied up there. There was a family of four on a small shabby little cabin cruiser, young parents in jeans, the girl with her hair tied back in a scarf, and two small boys in orange lifejackets. Behind them, and a considerable contrast, was a large, glossy and, even to Judith's untutored eyes, plainly expensive cruiser with a centre cockpit, a big deck aft covered in bright folding chairs, cushions and a table loaded with bottles and glasses, occupied by two middle-aged couples in well-pressed white trousers and navy blue blazers.

'Betcha they've got caps covered in gold braid,' Leo commented nastily. But as he spoke, his arm came round her shoulders in a most comforting way.

Water was gushing into the lock now, foaming past the prow of the little family cruiser and making it swing, while the water level rose steadily and the boats rose upwards. Behind the two cruisers was a traditional canal narrow boat, with flower paintings on bow and stern. Its occupants were young, and might have been a group of students from anywhere, the men bearded, the girls long-haired, all of them in jeans and shirts. A geranium in a pot stood on the cabin roof and a bunch of wildflowers in a jam jar was just visible through the double doors at the stern.

'You can hire those from any of the firms with marinas in the canal system,' Leo told her.

'What a gorgeous holiday it would make,' Judith said longingly.

To his astonishment, Leo heard himself promising her such a holiday, if she really wanted it. He listened to himself with considerable dismay. He must be right out of his mind. He, Leo Rosenstein, who throughout his days at the Central had steadfastly refused to set foot on any sort of boat, was planning to take Judith Chasemore on a boating – or even, worse still, a barging – holiday on the Thames. He didn't know what the hell he was up to today. Except for one thing. Life was great.

'Come along,' he said. 'We'll walk to the end of the island. Look at the view. Quite something, it is.'

The river wound down towards Richmond, weeping willows drooping on one shore, where there was a sheltered leafy walk, while on the other bank blocks of flats and houses were surrounded by wide lawns sweeping down to the water, ending often in stone steps leading to landing-stages.

Judith took a deep breath. 'Imagine living there. With a garden going down to the river, and a boat.'

This was it. This was what he'd wanted to hear. 'Back to the car,' he said smugly. 'Place I wanna show you.' He hustled her along and into the Mercedes, drove over a bridge and turned off along a road bordered by large old Victorian and Edwardian houses, blocks of flats, the occasional mellow Georgian mansion.

Leo passed one of these and pulled into a small drive. The house was a modern replica of a Georgian cottage. A low building of red brick and white-painted sash windows, with conifers screening it from the road and behind it a lawn and steps down to the water. Even at first glance, the house, though hardly more than about ten years old, already possessed the placid tranquillity of an established home.

'Me country cottage,' Leo announced. He eyed her narrowly.

Everyone at the Central knew about his country cottage, where, gossip had it, he took his lovely ladies for weekends.

'Me Mum's house, in fact,' he told her. 'When me Dad died – which he did comparatively early on – she wanted to move out of London but stay within reach of the Central, so I could keep on popping down. So I found 'er this place. It's built on what was the tennis court of the big 'ouse next door. She was 'appy 'ere, in spite of me Dad going so sudden. I could drive out from the Central, be 'ere under the 'alf 'our. Out of the rush-hour. It was the rush-hour that stopped me actually moving in with 'er, except when I 'ad a weekend off.'

'I can imagine she liked it here. It's so peaceful. And the river at the end of the garden.' Judith was dreamy, imagining herself living here with Leo. Their home. They'd have children and bring them up by the river, in and out of boats, in little orange lifejackets, by the time they could crawl. Hastily she pulled herself together. Daydreams were out. Reality was in. She was the latest in the long line of Leo's girlfriends. She was so lucky. But the story wouldn't end here. Not for her. She must face that squarely, and live for the moment. 'He who kisses the joy as it flies, lives in eternity's sunrise.'

She would kiss joy as it flew, not demand the moon and the stars and anything else that was going.

Leo was still telling her about his mother. 'Until she married me Dad,' he explained, 'she was a country girl. That was 'ow she met 'im. She came up, see, with her Dad, to Covent Garden – the fruit and vegetable market was still there, then – from the country down in Kent where they lived. And me Dad fell for her. Just like that, he told me. She was only about eleven when he first saw her, but he knew she was the girl he was going to marry. And he married her when she was sixteen and he was twenty-two.'

'Oh, Leo, what a lovely story.' Judith was immensely touched. The story was new to her, too. No one around the hospital had passed this piece of Leo's family history on to her. Hardly surprising, as he'd never told anyone of it before. But this she failed to guess.

'Go in, shall we?'

'Oh yes, please.' Judith was eager to see inside. Eager, too, to be included, as she imagined, among the string of girlfriends he'd brought here.

He unlocked the front door and took her into a spacious hall, where there was shining white paint, acres of warm golden carpet, and highly polished furniture.

'Like a cuppa?'

'I'd love one.' She followed him through a door at the rear of the hall into a shining kitchen. 'But will there be – '

'Everything to 'and.' He opened the refrigerator, took out milk, filled an electric kettle. 'Gotta caretaker. The housekeeper next door, from the big 'ouse we passed – it's flats now, matter of fact – she comes in and out, keeps the place aired and sees it stocked up with fresh food, so I can drop in when I want.' He made tea, found chocolate biscuits, and carried a tray through, Judith following with the kettle, to a room overlooking the river, filled with sofas and chairs and the same atmosphere of peace as the house had exuded from the first.

'What a lovely room. And a heavenly view.' Judith sipped the refreshing tea, and stared out of the window at the river. 'Your country cottage,' she mused. She was thinking how different it had turned out to be from anything she might have imagined.

'The caretaker won't disturb us, though.' Leo's thoughts had been following their own track. 'She knows when she sees the car that I want a bit of peace and quiet if I come down here, like to be left alone.'

Judith was filled, as she sat there in the pretty sitting-room drinking tea from his mother's flowery china, with admiration and affection for him, his family, his entire background. And with so much more. With a surging love and devotion that she was afraid was going to last for ever. But emotion, not for the first time, choked her, and all she gave him was a companionable grin. 'Oh yes, Leo,' she said airily. 'I bet she knows. And I bet she keeps away. After all, this is where you bring your lovely ladies, isn't it?' She stopped, aghast. She'd gone too far. She hadn't meant it to sound like that. Only Central gossip, no more, but she had appeared to accuse him of unmentionable orgies – here, in his mother's house.

She knew why the silly phrases had slipped out.

The thought of all these dashing, fashionable beauties
Leo had known and loved overwhelmed her. Beside
them she felt hopelessly inadequate. Even so, here she
was, lining up with them to her surprise and delight,
one in the long series. For how long she'd be able to
hold her place, whether this shining afternoon would
be the one and only occasion on which he brought her
here, she dared not think. She couldn't imagine how it
had come about that they were here at all, she and
Leo, and she had no clue as to how long their
companionship could last. Another hour or two? A
day or two? Even, was it possible, a month or two? She
prayed fervently that it might last for six months. Six
years. But she knew she'd be incredibly lucky if it
lasted six days. Whatever happened, though, today
was fantastic. But why had she risked throwing it all
away by making such a snide remark? Agitated, she
gulped scalding tea and wished she'd kept her mouth
shut.

'Wotcher mean, my lovely ladies?'

He sounded furious, but she'd said it, and even if
she wished she hadn't, she wasn't going to climb down
now. Anyway, it might be just as well. At least he'd be
reassured, understand she wasn't expecting any sort of
permanent relationship, nothing to embarrass him.
No hanging on.

She told him exactly what she'd meant.

He stared at her. 'Oh,' he said, his eyes travelling
up and down in a way that made her shiver. 'So that's
how you think of y'rself, is it?' Amazingly, he grinned
broadly. 'Once aboard the lugger and the girl is mine,
as me Dad used to say. Right, me girl, come 'ere and
blooming well be one of me lovely ladies.' He
beckoned her, in a manner he often used on a ward
round when he summoned a student to step forward

and examine a patient. 'Over 'ere, fast.'

Idiotically, she was in heaven. She put her teacup down in its saucer with enormous care, rose to her feet, and advanced tremulously across the carpet.

He took her into strong arms, and walked her out into the hall, up the wide staircase, and into a room that was unmistakably his own and nothing to do with his mother. He pulled back the bedspread, a faded, striped Indian cotton, and began to undress her with experienced loving hands. 'I've waited for this so long,' he said, to her astonishment. 'So very long.' His hands ran down her naked spine, and she shivered again. 'Lovely ladies, indeed,' he said. 'You're lovely, you know that? You're the loveliest thing I ever came across in me 'ole misspent existence.' He chuckled, and it was a heady sound that made her blood sing. 'But you've got a bloody cheek, me girl, you know that?' Suddenly he was sober. 'Let me tell you, little Miss Know-all, that I've never brought no one 'ere except you. This was me Mums' 'ome, and I've never brought a girl 'ere I wouldn't want 'er to meet.' His face dissolved into tragedy. 'And I only wish you and she could have met. She'd have taken to you, she would.'

It was the most perfect thing he could have said to her, and it gave her all the confidence she needed. She took his head between her two hands and kissed him with all the love that was in her.

## Chapter 8

When she awoke, he was no longer with her. She peered vaguely about the empty room, filled with old schoolbooks and photographs. A shabby room.

She had nothing but certainty, though. Wherever he was, he'd return to her.

Indolently, she lay back, allowed time to drift past, while dusk took over the shadowy room.

She didn't hear him on the stairs, but suddenly he was there. He was carrying a tray.

'Supper,' he said. 'Reckon you need it.'

He'd brought plates of mushroom omelette, hot brown rolls, and a pot of coffee. He put the tray down and settled cosily alongside her. 'Far too narrer for two, this bed. We'll have to see about it.' He handed her a plate of omelette. 'You look great in y'r skin.' He kissed her affectionately on her nose. 'But maybe you'd like a wrap of some sort?'

'I'm marvellously warm.'

'No, you'd better have something over your shoulders at least. Me old school blazer. 'Ow would that be?'

There could be only one thing better than sitting naked alongside Leo in bed, and that was to be enclosed in his old school blazer. She smiled hugely. 'Please.'

He fetched it from the wall cupboard, a faded worn garment, quite unlike the velvet jackets he affected in

his own flat, and she snuggled into it. Discovering she
was starving, she tucked into the omelette. It tasted
delicious.

'How on earth did you manage to find mushroom
omelette and hot rolls in an empty house? Did you
summon your caretaker, or what?'

'Nope. All in stock. The mushrooms are out of a tin,
and the rolls come vacuum packed. You pop them into
the oven for ten minutes, and they come out as you
see.' Buns in the oven, he thought, remembering a
crudity of his youth. It no longer seemed crude, but
instead full of hope. With this lovely, frail, wonderful
girl, he was going to raise a family. He kissed her
again, this time on her mouth, and cupped the firm
line of her breast under his blazer. 'You have ravishing
breasts,' he said. 'I use the word with some care.'

He sounded, all at once, as if he were on a teaching
round, and she spluttered with laughter. 'You're not
demonstrating me,' she reminded him.

'Not likely. No way. You're my private personal bit
of crumpet.' He frowned. Another expression from
early days. He ought not to have used it.

Judith didn't appear to object.

'And you're my personal private hunk of lovely
man,' she told him, pressing her hand hard against his
large and solid chest. 'Underneath all this hair I can,
just, feel your rib-cage. You ought to lose weight.'

'Dare say I will, if we go on like this for long enough.
All this exercise, and only omelette and coffee now and
then to keep us going.'

'We must have sweated pounds.'

'Drink up your coffee and we'll sweat some more.
You can regard it as a part of your campaign to slim
me.' He grinned wickedly, and his dark eyes were slits
of happiness, until all at once they changed, became

hungry and intent. 'So off with this old blazer and on your back, my lovely.'

Again they made love tempestuously, and again they slept.

They drove back to London alongside a river that gleamed and shone in the darkness.

'Wish we could have stayed until morning,' Leo said. 'But there's that damn rush-hour, and I can't afford to be late – me first teaching round since being in the States.'

'You'll be busy,' she agreed disconsolately, resigning herself to a day without him.

'Not too busy to 'ave supper with you. But lunch, even a sandwich, is another matter. We'd better not count on that.'

'No, I suppose not.'

He kissed her lingeringly, and sat in the Mercedes watching her enter her own block. His girl. His girl for ever.

In the morning he was as busy as he'd forecast. Even so, he found time to ring a jeweller in Hatton Garden. In the Central, it was a longstanding joke that what with his schoolfriends, his former patients, his friends from the greengrocery business, together with their assorted relatives, there was hardly a family in the city with whom Leo couldn't make personal contact if he wished. Today was no exception. He'd been at school with the jeweller, whom he asked to look out for a necklace with an emerald. 'Plain,' he instructed. 'With a narrow chain. Modern. And an emerald ring I want, too. Find a nice selection of rings, would ya, Izzy?'

Izzy, naturally, promised to do so. 'Shall I send them round? Or will you be stepping in?'

'Bit busy, I am. Bring 'em round one evening,

would you? Gimme a ring when you've got 'em, and
we'll make a date.'

Izzy made notes on his pad, and told his wife Leo
must be running a new girlfriend. 'Redhead, at a
guess.'

In the Central, though, they knew nothing of any
new girlfriend, redheaded or otherwise. They
assumed, on the contrary, that while he'd been in
America he'd picked up again with Melanie, and now
that he was back in the hospital he'd very likely run
Stella as a stand-in until Melanie's return. By now
they'd written off Sister Henderson, and none of them
spared a glance for Judith, whom they'd begun to take
for granted as they'd been in the habit of taking
Sophie for years.

What they did think was that he looked amazingly
tired, but that he'd obviously recovered his spirits. At
least his trip had done that for him. Melanie must go
deeper than they'd realised. He'd been missing her,
that was why he'd been so impossible recently.

All of them had a busy day, and none of them raised
an eyebrow when he carted Judith off to his flat for
supper. He hadn't yet had a chance to catch up on his
paperwork.

It was not, of course, paperwork that he and Judith
caught up on, and when she awoke the next morning —
in her own bed, where she had returned in the small
hours — she was so enfolded in happiness that she was
ready to explode.

Instead, she breakfasted decorously with her father,
and went along to Harley Street where, dotingly, she
typed letters and case notes from Leo's dictation the
previous day, dwelling lovingly on every changing
timbre of his voice even as it came, metallic and
altered, off the cassettes.

At lunchtime, making the excuse to herself – but not taking herself in – that he'd like to sign his letters and get them off, she took his correspondence over to the hospital, knowing perfectly well that her true reason was an overwhelming urge to take advantage of the slim chance of setting eyes on him again before the evening. She'd leave his letters in the surgeon's rest-room, and he'd be able to sign them between operations, or at the end of his list.

She went into the surgical block and up in the fast lift. In the surgeons' rest-room alongside the general theatre, she placed the little pile ready on the table by the chair he normally used. Had she any reason whatever for hanging around waiting for him?

If she went along to the anaesthetic room, of course, they'd know how the list was going, and they'd be able to tell her if it would be worth her while to wait. But on the other hand, once she'd put in an appearance there, she'd have no excuse for sticking around if they told her he'd be hours yet.

Uncertain, she dithered. If she remained where she was, went in search of no one, simply stayed here until he finally emerged from the theatre, she could always pretend she'd only just walked in with his letters. No one would know how long she'd been there.

In the general theatre they'd found Leo difficult this morning, something they hadn't expected. Where had all yesterday's bonhomie gone?

Jeremy Hillyard, who had been playing a lot of tennis that summer, was once again boring them with details of the tournament he and his partner had so nearly won, when Leo walked in, plainly in a bit of a temper. Jeremy hastily abandoned the tale of his near-triumph, though not before Leo had grasped the drift of his remarks.

'Tennis, is it?' he enquired, an edge to his voice they failed to understand. Indeed, he didn't understand it himself. All right, so it was not now a game Judith could play, but surely he could hear it mentioned without losing his cool? Why in God's name should he want so fiercely to demolish the inoffensive Jeremy merely because he happened to have been playing a bit of that amazingly boring game? 'Let's see,' he heard himself say nastily, 'if you can produce some more purposeful dexterity in the service of suffering 'umanity for a change, shall we?'

Over masks, eyes met. The chief was in a hell of a mood.

Everyone around him became quietly efficient and astonishingly taciturn, while Leo, a good deal to their surprise, since operating even under the most baffling circumstances usually put him into a genial and expansive frame of mind, remained tight-lipped and snappish.

They were halfway through the list, just about to begin a partial gastrectomy, when out of the blue he asked Stella to have someone fetch him his Rennies from the pocket of his jacket hanging in his locker.

'Of course, sir. Nurse Hall.'

'Yes, Sister. At once.'

'Thank you, Sister.'

Once more, eyes were meeting. So that was what it was. The great man had an ordinary attack of indigestion. Been eating too well again. Hangover, too, very likely.

Leo, who, as usual, was well aware of the line their thoughts were following, hoped they were right.

He'd been feeling tired and off-colour all morning. At first he'd pushed the fatigue and the queasiness to the back of his mind, determined to ignore them. All right, he'd been overdoing it. So what? He was fit, wasn't he?

He was beginning to wonder if he was. And that pain that he'd put down to a bit of stiffness after swimming was radiating now up into the back of his neck and jaw, setting his teeth on edge.

He could diagnose himself easily enough. There were two possibilities, and he settled, typically, for the more optimistic. Everyone, not Judith alone, was for ever telling him he ought to lose weight. Instead, in the States, with all that ceaseless hospitality, he'd been putting it on. This pain was almost certainly caused by a hiatus hernia, the reflux of acid from his stomach up into his gullet. Rennies would cure it, as they'd done in the past.

When Nurse Hall returned with his carton of the small peppermint-flavoured tablets he chewed one and waited for the pain to go away. It didn't, so he took another, and got on with the job.

While he and Nick and Jeremy carried on with the gastrectomy, the pain stayed with him. He and Nick spoke little – they'd worked together for so many years now they knew the requirements of any operation they did as if they were instrumentalists in a long-established orchestra playing a familiar score almost automatically. Today, though, Leo was beginning to thank whatever lucky stars remained to him that Nick was here, not Jeremy alone. If the pain got much worse, he'd safely be able to leave the two of them to continue.

They were coming towards the end of the main procedure of resecting the stomach and providing a new working anatomical arrangement. It should be plain sailing now – and if it wasn't, Nick would be able to cope. Leo was becoming more and more aware that he wasn't going to be able, himself, to finish. But Nick had done it many times, starting years back under Leo's supervision.

The pain was a good deal worse, and he began at last to worry more about himself than the surgery, forced to recognise that this was no hiatus hernia. His first diagnosis had been wrong. The second, far more dangerous possibility was the correct deduction. He had the pain not only in his jaw, but right across his chest. Soon he felt a weight on his chest. This was it. The classic tag slipped menacingly into his consciousness. 'An elephant sitting on his chest.' A symptom of coronary thrombosis, a heart attack.

That was what was happening to him. He was having a coronary.

Round him, as they worked, the eyes above the masks were worried. This was no joke. Indigestion was out. The chief was ill. Each of them was sure of it, and in split seconds when they could spare the fraction of their attention, worried glances crossed, doubtful eyes dwelt anxiously on Leo. Nick rehearsed a form of words which would order Leo out of his own theatre, force him to seek medical aid. Still, though, he hesitated. Would Leo go? Or would he stay to argue? That would help no one – not the patient on the table, not Leo himself. And, Nick knew, in this predicament, his first duty was not to Leo, but to the patient. The patient was anaesthetised, had surrendered mind and body in trust to their care. He had to come first.

Leo was certain now. He knew what he was facing. Nick would have to complete the operation.

'I think you'll have to finish this on your own, Nick,' he growled, in a surly disagreeable voice.

This time, though, none of them misunderstood. This was not irritability or impatience. This was a man desperate with pain.

'I'm going out for a few minutes,' he ended. He walked away from the table.

Nick looked straight across at him. He didn't at all care for what little he could see of Leo himself, above his mask and below his surgical cap. His skin was pale, sweating and with a blue tinge to it. The lobes of his ears were mauve. His breathing was bad, and as he walked off, Nick could see his chest heaving beneath the crumpled green blood-spattered surgical gown.

He didn't, however, allow his eyes to follow Leo. His own commitment was to complete the operation.

'Now, Jeremy,' he said. 'You and I have to finish this gastrectomy. You take over from me here.' He strode round the table, taking Leo's position next to Stella, his concentration locked into the next stage of the surgery. Just before he started, though, he looked up at Stella. 'Sister, I thought Mr Rosenstein looked very poorly indeed – would you send someone along to see if he's all right?'

'Of course,' Stella said. Her brown eyes signalled across to Nurse Hall, who nodded and said, 'Yes, Sister, at once,' and left the theatre. 'I thought so too,' Stella added, her eyes coming back to Nick's – but meeting only the back of his capped head as he leant over the operation site.

Judith, hovering indecisively in the surgeon's room, heard someone coming slowly along in squeaking theatre boots. She straightened up, wondering who it could be – someone breathing heavily, with difficulty, and walking very slowly.

As he walked in, green-gowned and bloodstained, she could hardly believe that this was indeed Leo. She'd been prepared for some unknown old man to appear. But it was Leo.

He caught sight of her.

'Jude,' he said. 'I feel awful. I think … must be having a coronary.'

In a wild rush across the room she reached him just as he lay down on the floor, and eased him as gently as she could to the cold tiles.

'Need admission, stat,' he muttered. 'Get hold of someone.'

Bending over him, she saw his terrible colour and caught her breath. He was in a bad way, and she ached with love and shared pain. What she had to do, though, was keep her head and get organised. 'Shall I ring for James Leyburn? Or – ?'

She saw that Leo hadn't even heard her question. His face was drained of colour now, and he was unconscious, she thought. She felt for his pulse, holding his big wrist in her hand, feeling and finding nothing. She tried next for the big artery in the neck. No pulse there, either.

At that point, to her amazed relief, Nurse Hall materialised from the theatre.

'Nurse,' Judith said, her voice, to her own surprise, coming out calm, clear and collected, 'Mr Rosenstein's arrested, I think. Call the cardiac resuscitation team on 181, will you?'

Nurse Hall would, and did. She went to the wall telephone, dialled, and spoke to whoever answered. 'Cardiac arrest,' she said. 'Surgeons' rest room, general theatre. Mr Rosenstein's arrested.'

By now Judith, like a good physiotherapist, had thumped Leo hard in the chest. Still no heartbeat, and she began direct cardiac massage.

Nurse Hall came over to join her. 'Airway clear?' she asked.

'Yes.'

Together, the two of them went into the drill they'd both been taught early in their training, mouth-to-mouth breathing and massage of the heart, until the rattle of trolley wheels and the stampede of feet announced the arrival of the resuscitation team. Suddenly the small room was full of people.

'This the patient?'

'Yes,' Judith snapped, exasperated. Did they suppose the room to be littered with supine bodies in green theatre gowns having coronaries, one in every corner?

'Right. Stand back, will you? How long's he been out?'

'Just under two minutes.'

'Right. You can leave him to us now. That's it.'

The figure she loved so much vanished from her sight entirely, surrounded by the busy resuscitation team and their apparatus. 'Can you get a pulse?' she heard.

Leo, she thought fiercely, Leo, do you hear me? I'm right beside you, so don't you dare go and die on me. Don't you dare. Stay alive, do you understand? Damn well stay alive.

She couldn't be going to lose him, could she? Not now, just when life had been going to be so terrific?

Leo, damn well stay alive.

# Chapter 9

Judith came down in the fast lift from intensive care in the cardiothoracic department, where the resuscitation team had taken Leo. She walked unseeingly through the hall of the tower block and out into the street. The day that had opened in such radiance had turned to black despair.

No. Not despair. She must never allow the word so much as house-room on the edge of her mind. Hope was the password.

For Leo was still alive.

But only just.

There was nothing she could do to help him – other than to refrain from hanging around, getting under everyone's feet and making a nuisance of herself. But how was she going to fill her time?

Her feet apparently knew the answer to this one. They had already taken her unerringly to Leo's orange Mercedes, sitting neatly in his parking space, where she'd left it when she arrived at the hospital with his letters.

His letters.

Waiting to be signed still, in the surgeons' rest-room in general surgery. She'd have to go and fetch them. She'd have to go back into that room where it had all happened.

She put the car keys back in her pocket, and set off for the tower block again. Back into the lift, out at

general surgery, and along to the theatres and
changing-rooms. Just don't think, don't remember,
don't relive it. Simply go in and pick up his letters and
go out again.

There they were, on the table where she'd put them,
at what she'd supposed would be the side of his
armchair. Don't think about him sitting in the
armchair talking and joking, as he'd done so many
times. Don't think about him treading slowly like an
old, old man along the passage and collapsing almost
into her arms. And then stopping breathing. Don't
think about it. Pick up the letters and leave.

She took the letters and retraced her steps. Back to
the lift, down again to the hall, and out into the open
air. Walk to the Mercedes, unlock the door, put the
letters and her sling bag down on the passenger seat.
Drive out of the Central and along to Leo's own
parking meter in Harley Street.

Work was the order of the day. Something had to be
done about these letters, and about Leo's
appointments. And Sophie would have to be told what
had happened, too. So she would let herself into
Harley Street, and go up and tell Sophie, calmly and
without fuss. Sophie would be upset in any case, so in
no way was she, Judith, going to burst in on her in
floods of tears and bawl out her story.

Judith was very much her father's daughter as she
rang the bell of the flat at the top of the house. Cool
and reserved. Practical.

'Sophie, I'm afraid I – '

'I know. Nick just telephoned. Isn't it horrible?'

Judith nodded.

'I can't bear it,' Sophie said. 'Darling Leo – a
coronary. I – he – he's like part of the family. Hell, I
feel so miserable. Oh, well,' she pushed her hair out of

her eyes and set her lips. She was showing her pregnancy now, no longer the lissome slight figure so familiar round the Central for years as Leo's secretary, but a sturdy blonde in a Laura Ashley smock, she seemed domestic and a bit lost. She opened her mouth and demonstrated she was nothing of the sort. 'God knows when I'll see Nick again. He'll be rushed off his feet, doing Leo's work and rearranging everything. And you'll be the same, so I'll come down and help out. What's the time?' She didn't wait for an answer, but glanced at her own wristwatch, 'Lunch first,' she said. 'You come in, Judy, and we'll have some soup and cheese together. We can plan while we eat, and then we'll go down to the office, and take turns at the telelphone and the typewriter. Lucky, with his operating list this morning, he had no patients to see here this afternoon, so there's no one to be put off in a rush.'

'Yes, a good thing,' Judith agreed automatically, though she didn't think anything today could be designated lucky. Just less awful.

She followed Sophie into her pretty kitchen, flowery walls and curtains, pine wall cupboards, table and chairs.

'We'll have a nourishing soup,' Sophie said. 'We're going to need our strength. How about lentil and tomato?'

'Lovely,' Judith said, trying to summon up enthusiasm.

'This is as good as a square meal,' Sophie said, stirring busily. 'I often make it for Nick at all hours. I've fed it into Leo on occasion, too. Oh dear.' She sniffed, blew her nose on a tissue, set her lips. 'You know, Nick and I both thought he looked whacked when we met him at Heathrow. We were worried

about him then. It was so unlike him to arrive home
flaked out after a lecture tour – usually he thrives on
them, and comes back bursting with ideas and energy
and go.'

Judith felt worse than ever. She thought of the day
following Leo's return, the packed day of joy and
excitement and heady rapture. Hardly a quiet day of
rest for a surgeon with jet-lag. Had she added to Leo's
exhaustion, been partly responsible herself for
bringing about this coronary attack?

Sophie poured the contents of her saucepan into two
pottery bowls and grated a mound of cheese on top.
'Right,' she said, sitting down at the table. 'Let's get
outside this, as Leo would say – the old sweetie, let's
*pray* for him – ' She screwed her eyes up tightly as she
said this, so Judith decided she must mean it literally,
and found she was pressing her own nails into her
palms and was repeating in her head, 'Please, God,
make Leo better. Please, God, make Leo better. Make
him better. Don't let him die.'

She pressed her lips together and stared across the
table at Sophie, who opened her own green eyes at
that moment and stared straight back. 'You have to do
something,' Sophie said almost apologetically. 'And
you never know, it might do some good. Think positive
thoughts – and get on with the job. That's our
attitude. Today's motto, as dreamed up by me, Sophie
Waring. Soph Waring, I should say.' Her face
crumpled, but again she set her lips. 'I am not going to
burst into tears and howl like a child. I'm going to eat
my lunch and come down into the office with you and
put in a good afternoon's work, like the sweet man
would expect.'

Judith nodded. Jude, she was thinking. Soph and
Jude. Two hideous names Leo had saddled them with,

and here they were, she and Sophie, ready to weep the afternoon away simply remembering that he was in the habit of calling them that. Live, Leo, live, damn you. She found she could, after all, swallow Sophie's soup. She had several mouthfuls and thought perhaps she'd better try to be a bit conversational, not leave it all to Sophie – who must be as upset as she was herself. Sophie had worked for Leo for years, ever since she'd come to the Central, and while she, Judith, might secretly love him, until a month ago she'd hardly known him.

'Pretty kitchen you have,' she said at random, and managed to produce a grin. 'Changing the subject,' she explained. 'Better for our digestions, I was thinking.'

'Better in every way. We can't sit about being miserable like this. Yes. The kitchen. Yes, it is nice, I think. I enjoy being in it. I'm planning the nursery now, for – ' her face crumpled again, and she swore as vehemently as any surgeon over the operating table. 'Sorry. But all roads seem to lead to Leo, and I can't bear it. For young Tobias, Leo's future godson, I was about to say. Because that's how he's been labelled for months. Hell, he's going to be Leo's godson, too.'

'Of course he is. Tell me about the nursery.'

'I'm painting it yellow – it doesn't get much sun. Only first thing in the morning. So I thought we wouldn't go in for blue for a boy or pink for a girl, but have a nice cheerful yellow-and-white room. Yellow walls and yellow rugs, and a lovely country-style curtain material I've discovered, wild flowers on a white ground, very fresh and pretty.'

'It sounds terrific,' Judith said, trying hard to whip up enthusiasm.

'It is nice.' Sophie's heart wasn't in it, either. 'Coffee

now, good and strong,' she suggested, 'and then we'll go downstairs and put our tiny noses to the grindstone.'

'I'd love some coffee.' Judith dragged her thoughts forcibly away from the coffee she and Leo drank at breakfast in his flat after their swim.

Sophie made her coffee in a machine on the pine dresser, and gave it to Judith in a pottery mug. While they were drinking it the telephone rang. Nick.

'I'll go on down and get a bit sorted out,' Judith said hastily. 'I'll take my coffee with me.' She left Sophie talking to Nick in the kitchen – like Leo, Sophie and Nick had telephones all over their flat, in the kitchen and bathroom as well as in the bedroom and sitting room. No doubt they'd soon have one installed in the nursery.

Downstairs in the office, Judith studied the appointments book. Some patients were regular attenders, and could easily be telephoned and put off temporarily. Others were new, and could only be reached through their family doctor. She'd begin with the straightforward calls, and have those out of the way first, she decided.

Sophie came in. 'Nick won't be back until late,' she said. 'They're having a big meeting of everyone in general surgery, to decide who'll do what. The consultants are coming in. So I told him I'd be down here helping you, and he said he thought we ought to put off all the patients we can this week, and those we can't put off either he or Aubrey Everard' – he was the junior consultant in the department – 'will have to see for him.'

Judith nodded.

'So if you ring round tomorrow's appointments and simply put them off, I'll go through the week in the diary, and try to pick out the ones who can't be put off. Are you doing anything this evening, or could you stay on?'

Judith wasn't doing anything. In fact, she was relieved at the necessity to stay on and work. She was afraid to be alone, remembering and worrying.

'That's all right, then.' Sophie was pleased. 'We can just carry on until all hours if we have to.'

'Did Nick say anything about how Leo is?'

'He's spoken to James Leyburn. James says Leo is still very poorly.' Sophie frowned. 'Very poorly' was an ominous phrase – it sometimes meant dying. 'But he says at the moment he'd holding his own. Only his heart is finding it hard work – this is what he told Nick – Leo's heart is finding it hard work to do even the minimal job of keeping his circulation going while he's lying in bed. He's on oxygen.'

'At least he's still with us,' Judith said. 'It's not much, but it's something.'

Sophie met her eyes. 'He's survived so far. We must hang on to that thought.'

After a bried pause while they both considered this, they turned back, by unspoken mutual agreement, to the desk littered with messages, letters, cassettes, the appointments book, the address book and the telephone directories with the medical directories.

The afternoon disappeared. Nick rang through again and advised sending out those of Leo's letters that were already on tape, perhaps with an extra paragraph explaining that Leo himself might not be able to see the patient in the immediate future, but that one of his colleagues would be happy to do so.

They drank tea and assessed how far they'd got.

'There are all this lot, to be rung this evening after six – mainly GPs, of course.'

'And then there are people like Lord Mummery, who'll have to be told – we can't leave him to find out on the grapevine. I wonder if anyone ought to tell that actress of Leo's, in the States?'

'Melanie,' Judith supplied gloomily.

'That's right. I suppose someone ought to let her know.'

Judith could think of nothing useful to say. Leo had told her a good deal about Melanie, but none of it had any connection with the possibility of ringing her up and informing her he'd had a coronary. Would she think she ought to fly home to be at his bedside? Would he want that? Certainly she, Judith, would hate it. But thoughts like this must be pushed away. If Leo would want Melanie he ought to have her, in case – she shook her head ferociously. That thought, too, had to be pushed away. But if Leo was ill, say, would he then prefer, instead of a new and untried love, the familiar Melanie, whom he'd known for ever?

Sophie, unaware of Judith's self-torment, put Melanie's name down on her list.

Judith began reading the diary for the coming month, and in the course of doing this, a subsidiary list emerged, of yet more friends or colleagues who would need to be told what had happened. There were apologies, too, to be sent to the chairmen of a vast number of committees. Soon Judith and Sophie were swamped by assorted lists.

Sophie stretched. 'We need a list of our lists,' she said. 'But at least we know now what we have to get through, and that's a step in the right direction. So how about if I leave you to sort out the priorities on all these revolting little pieces of paper, while I put some food into the oven, and then I'll come down again and we'll tackle the evening calls to the GPs?'

'Fine. Before you go, though, can you make me up a nice extra paragraph for all these letters? Then I can begin doing them in between telephone calls.'

'Sure. Let's think. "Unfortunately, I shan't be able to see – or operate on, or look after, or whatever – this patient myself in the next week or two – "'

'*Week* or two? Surely – '

'I know. Better say that, though. We can't plan for months ahead at this stage. This is only a holding measure. Um – so "week or two, but one of my colleagues will be happy to look after him or her in the short term. Perhaps you'd let my secretary know what arrangements you'd like made, and she will fix up Mr or Mrs Whoever-they-are in whatever way you would like. I am so sorry not to be able to look after him, stroke her, myself." Then you put "dictated by Mr Rosenstein and signed in his absence, Jude Chasemore, Sec." .'

Jude Chasemore, Sec. Judith felt like dying. Instead, she said, 'Thanks, Soph. I'm OK now, so you get up them stairs and start the slaving over a hot stove bit, while I hit the typewriter.'

Brave words, but they led to her undoing. She began running the tapes, and Leo's fruity voice threw her completely. To sit in the office listening to it, hear him commenting on patients, throwing in little asides for her ear alone, to sit and listen to this, and know he might be dying, she might never see him again – she put her head down on the typewriter and howled.

But then she sat back, straightened her shoulders, blew her nose and mopped at her damp face. She restarted the tapes and typed the letters. What she didn't do was wipe them clean. Instead, hoping Sophie would never discover what she'd done, she secreted them in her bag.

Sophie's casserole was comforting. Chicken and mushroom, with potatoes baked in their jackets and fresh green beans. Both of them were ravenously hungry, and very tired – they'd talked their heads off on the telephone all evening, since they'd left messages at any number of surgeries, and family doctors seemed to ring them back at five-minute intervals from all over the country.

The telephone continued to ring while they ate. They took it in turns to answer it. The message pad filled up. Sophie made coffee in her machine.

'You'd better pack it in and go home now,' she suggested. 'You've done enough, and tomorrow's bound to be another frantic day. If you leave the lists here, I'll go through them with Nick when he comes in.'

Judith was uncertain. 'What about the telephone?' she asked. 'I'm afraid it's going to ring all evening.'

Sophie grinned – the first genuine grin she'd produced that day. 'I'm used to that.'

At that point Nick walked in. He looked even more tired than they felt, and Judith would have slipped away, leaving him to what peace he and Sophie might be able to snatch together, but he greeted her noisily.

'Look who's here,' he bellowed. 'The girl of the moment.'

Judith was puzzled. 'Me?' she asked. 'Why? What have I done?'

'Only saved Leo's life, for God's sake.' Nick, usually rather quiet and self-contained, was explosive, hugged Judith and lifted her off her feet.

'How is Leo?' she began to ask, but Sophie talked her down.

'Saved Leo's life? Judy did? You never said.' She glared accusingly. 'Here we've been all day, almost, and you never said a word. What happened?'

'Well, I – '

'The entire hospital – or at any rate the whole of general surgery and the cardiothoracic department – are singing her praises. Seriously, though, Judith, it was immensely well done. We all recognise it. If it hadn't been for you, I think he'd very likely be dead, you know.'

'Someone tell me what all this is about,' Sophie said firmly. 'Nick darling, Judy hasn't breathed a word about any of this. So tell me from the beginning. What happened?'

'Nothing much,' Judith said hastily. 'It was just that I was in the surgeons' room when he came out of the theatre and so I sort of fielded him, and – '

'And resuscitated him.' Nick was emphatic. 'James Leyburn says that when the cardiac arrest team arrived you had him breathing again.'

Judith nodded soberly. 'Yes, he had a pulse again, and he was breathing.' Reliving the moment, she paled.

'He came into the surgeons' room, did he?' Sophie asked. 'All this is new to me.'

'It happened so quickly.' Judith felt apologetic. 'And it didn't seem important. The cardiac team took him over, and rushed him off. I was only in at the beginning, nothing more.'

'A good deal more.' Nick was determined. 'You were there when he arrested, you took the emergency measures. They were sucessful. If you hadn't been there, or if you hadn't reacted effectively, he wouldn't be alive now. That's a lot more than nothing, and we all recognise it.'

'You mean he arrested at your feet?' Sophie asked.

'He was at the other side of the room,' Judith told

her. 'He said "Jude".' She had to stop, as she relived
the moment. 'He looked terrible, a dreadful colour,
and his breathing was so laboured. I was appalled.
And he said "I think I'm having a coronary," or
something like that, and then he went down. On to the
floor. I'd reached him by then, so I sort of broke his
fall a bit, and he said "Get someone", and then he
went out like a light. I felt for his pulse, and it wasn't
there. I couldn't get a carotid pulse either. So I
thumped him in the chest, and gave him cardiac
massage.'

'Thus saving his life, as I've pointed out.' Nick
looked across at Sophie.

'I couldn't have managed if that dark nurse from the
theatre hadn't arrived just then. She rang for the
resuscitation team, and then she came over and gave
him the massage, to relieve me, while I did the mouth-
to-mouth breathing. And we got a pulse back.' She
remembered the one good moment in a dreadful day.

'You deserve a brandy,' Nick said. 'At least. And so
do I, as a matter of fact, though for more mundane
reasons. And so does Sophie, but she, poor love, won't
get one.' He kissed his wife.

'Lovely old orange juice for me,' she agreed. 'But if
you're going to have brandy, does that mean you're
finished for the day? No more calls?'

'No more calls. Aubrey Everard has turned up
trumps for once. He said I'd borne the brunt of the
day, and he'd take the calls from now on. Jeremy's on
first call, and anything he can't handle alone he's
referring to Aubrey. All I have left to do is ring Lord
Mummery. And I need a brandy before I cope with
him.'

'Oh, you're doing that, are you?' Sophie asked, and
reached for the lists, now held together by a bulldog

clip.

'Got landed with it. After all, I was his houseman once. Must say I'm dreading it. The old boy is going to be upset – he's very fond of Leo.'

'What's the latest on Leo himself?'

Judith was thankful to hear Sophie make the enquiry. She'd been asking herself at what stage she could butt in with a question about Leo's exact condition.

'Holding his own. Poorly still. Prognosis – who can say?'

Sophie nodded.

'Point in his favour,' Nick went on, 'and James Ley burn agrees with me, is that he's naturally tough. A survivor, you might say. Other than that, there's nothing particularly hopeful. James says we must plan for him to be off for a minimum of six weeks, even if all goes well. Duties have been allocated on that basis, and we're to have a locum in his place.'

'A locum? You mean a consultant?' Sophie put down her orange juice with a crash. 'But surely you'll take over Leo's work?'

'Some of it needs a consultant.'

'But you could have had a consultant post any day in the past few years, outside the Central. And you know the work and the department and – and everything. They can't possibly find anyone nearly as good as you. Do you mean to say – ?'

'Calm down, love. They might. All depends who puts in. Must admit, I'd been supposing – when I had time to think about anything except what I was doing, and the next job after it – I'd assumed that somehow I'd go on minding the shop for Leo until he was fit to do it himself again.'

'That's what he'd want.'

'I think it is. But he's not in a position to say. And no one's going to badger him about it. Or about the department at all. That's our priority. All I hope is we don't get landed with Robinson.'

'Robinson? Oh, *no,*' Sophie shut her eyes and moaned. 'Surely you couldn't be stuck with *him?*'

'Well, he's around. He's always around. And qualified. He has his Fellowship and his Master's degree neatly stashed away, even if he is a bit of a butcher, in my personal opinion, not to mention easily the rudest oaf around the hospital, in everyone's opinion.'

'You can't have him in the department.' Sophie was outraged.

'I certainly hope not. But it occurred to me – only after the meeting, or I might have done something about it – that it would be exactly like him to weasel his way into Leo's job.'

'You never ought to have let them decide to look for a locum at all.' Sophie was clear in her mind. 'You should have said at once that you could handle everything, and asked for a registrar to assist you.'

'That's what I should have done,' Nick agreed. 'But I didn't. You know how it is at a meeting. If you don't seize the moment, it's too late, the situation has got away from you. When the question came up, I was too busy thinking about who would do what, and for how long, to realise the implications.'

'And you were tired too, I expect,' Sophie told him. 'That's when things like that slip past.'

'We're all tired. I prescribe bed. Tomorrow is another day. Judith, can I run you home?'

'No, don't bother. Only a step, after all. And the fresh air will clear my head.'

'Are you sure?' Nick, though plainly hoping not to have to turn out again, was persistent.

'Absolutely. See you tomorrow. 'Bye.' She went out of the room, downstairs, through the big front door and into Harley Street. There on Leo's parking space stood the Mercedes, and she gave it an affectionate pat as she went by. Part of her life with Leo. Her brief, short delirium of joy, swept away so abruptly.

# Chapter 10

When Judith let herself into her own flat, her father, unusually for him, came out into the hall to greet her.

'I'm proud of you,' he said. 'They're all saying you were responsible for keeping Leo alive until the resuscitation team took over. You did well.'

'I just happened to be there.' Judith didn't want to discuss Leo with her father. Too much would have to be left unsaid – and in any case, she found she was averse to listening to his comments on the day's events. But then she recollected Nick and Sophie's alarm over the appointment of a locum consultant. Fed up she might be, and tired as well. But the day was not, after all, over. Her father could be useful.

'You were at the meeting, then, were you, Dad?'

'That's right. We were all there, trying to sort things out.'

'I heard something about a locum consultant.'

'We decided to advertise for one – all we can do, in the circumstances.'

'Leo,' Judith was firm, 'would have wanted Nick Waring to handle his work. After all, he's a very senior senior registrar, only there because he doesn't want a consultant post outside the Central.'

'True enough. But he has the administration of the department on his shoulders. Fellow can't do everything.'

'It won't help him to have a strange consultant there, learning the ropes.'

'That's true. It won't. He'd have to go round with him, explaining it all – the patients, our methods, and so on. That would add to his problems, I agree. But only in the short term. Anyway, he said nothing against the plan. If he didn't care for it, he could have spoken up. Got a tongue in his head.'

'And a good deal on his mind.'

'That's so.'

'You don't think it might be an idea if he was appointed as the locum consultant?' Judith tried to sound her most uncertain and tentative, thoroughly unsure of herself – which was not how she was feeling. 'People are saying he could have had a consultant post years ago, if he hadn't been waiting for the general surgery post in the hospital when Stephen King retires.'

'That's not a bad idea, I must say.' Her father seemed quite struck by the suggestion.

She threw out her next comment even more cautiously. 'What people seem to be expecting – I dare say they're quite wrong – is that Robinson will get the post.'

This statement produced almost the same effect on her father as it had on Sophie.

'Robinson? Did you say Robinson?' He shut his eyes, just as Sophie had done. Evidently the picture called up was too distasteful to be faced. 'We can't have that sewer in general surgery. Only make matters worse, and they're already bad enough.' He was decisive. 'Unthinkable.'

'People are saying it would be typical of him to infiltrate himself now, and stay for ever.'

Her father emitted a short sharp bark, which was

unlike him, but entirely comprehensible to anyone who knew Robinson.

'He's a fast worker when he needs to be, as well as sly,' Judith pointed out, herself exercising both those qualities with consummate skill. 'And of course on paper he has all the right qualifications.'

'So has Nick.' Her father was sharp.

'Well, yes, but – '

'Ought to have put himself forward. However, I can understand why he didn't, in the circumstances. Mistake, though.'

'Yes, I can see it was.' Judith did her best to look helpless and worried to death, though at that precise moment her feelings were quite other.

'Not to worry.' Her father was suddenly genial. 'Leave it to me. I'll see to it. Glad you mentioned it.' He went into the sitting-room, and picked up the telephone.

'I'll have my bath,' Judith remarked to the well-tailored back as the telephone dial spun.

'Get off to bed, yes.' Her father had lost interest in her, and his voice was vague. 'You must be tired. Ah, is that you, Aubrey? Rob here. Sorry to disturb you at this hour, but a point has just occurred to me, and I thought it might be useful if we had a word. Thing is ...'

Judith went off to her bath, and then to bed. She was so tired she fell asleep at once, and when she awoke next morning there was no chance to lie about feeling miserable. She had promised to join Sophie in Harley Street as early as possible, so she dressed, made herself a cup of instant coffee, and departed.

Early as it was, she found Sophie in the office, sorting out the lists and the messages. 'Hi,' she said. 'Nick went over to the cardiothoracic department at

first light, more or less, to try and catch James
Leyburn before his operating list, to see what he
thinks of Leo.'

'Have you heard anything?'

'Only that he's still with us, praise be. Nick's
hoping to be able to see him today.'

This remark jerked Judith into unexpected pain.
Was there any chance that she herself might be able to
see Leo? Go in and sit by his bed, hold his hand in her
own? She fought the thought down – though she
would have done better to have raised it, and to have
come clean about her own feelings for Leo. Instead,
she postponed the issue. After Nick had seen Leo, she
decided, she might be able to put forward the
possibility of going in and seeing him herself.

'Lord Mummery is talking of coming up next week,'
Sophie informed her, a glint in her eyes. 'He says he
can see a few patients, sort them out for us. He says
he'll do Leo's outpatients and see patients here as
well, two afternoons a week.' The green eyes snapped.
'That'll make something to tell the GPs – they won't
have to be fobbed off with a mere senior registrar.' She
was sarcastic.

'I told my father what we'd been thinking about
Robinson,' Judith told her. 'He seemed to think he
could soon put a stop to anything like that, and he
rang up Aubrey Everard last night, after I got home.'

'Wow,' Sophie said. 'You don't let the grass grow,
do you? First of all, you resuscitate Leo – you might
have told me about that, I do think – and then you
stop awful Robinson in his tracks. Nick was really
quite depressed about him. We ought to have had you
around the department years ago. I suppose you
wouldn't care to organise Nick into the consultant
post as well, would you?'

Judith was uncertain whether or not to tell her that she hoped she had achieved exactly that – but what if it didn't come off?

The telephone put a stop to their discussion.

Meanwhile, over in the hospital, Nick caught James Leyburn doing an early round in intensive care.

'Got a minute?'

'Sure.' With his big frame and his plain, gentle face, after twenty years at the Central James Leyburn still looked more like a West Country farmer than a leading heart surgeon, and his voice carried traces of the soft Somerset burr. Though no one could move faster when necessary, he was seldom seen in any apparent hurry, and he showed no impatience now, though his list was impending. 'You want to hear about Leo, is that it?'

'That's right. How's he going along?'

'Still very poorly. Not in pain, though. Rather breathless, in spite of the oxygen. The drugs are holding his cardiac rhythm satisfactorily so far, but I must say we're going to be more or less counting every beat for the next week.'

Nick nodded, looking as depressed as he felt.

'You needn't be afraid we're not pulling out all stops,' James went on, trying to be reassuring. 'We're getting superb laboratory back-up, I must say, and if human effort and skill can keep him going and get him back on his feet, it's all there. But, at the moment, as I say, he's still very poorly. Would you like to look in on him?'

'What do you think?'

'I should think he'd be glad to see you. Hear from your own mouth that everything's under control in his department – presumably you can tell him that?' The normally kind eyes were probing.

'No problem. Everything taken care of – other than Lord Mummery's threatened arrival to supervise us all. But that might cheer Leo no end, even if it is putting the fear of God into me.'

'Right. In you go.' James jerked his head towards the third door on the left.

Leo was propped up in bed, on oxygen still, as James had said. His skin was pale, and his lips had an unwelcome blue tinge. His breathing was slightly laboured, Nick noticed at once, and altogether he didn't much care for the look of him.

'Huh,' Leo said, eyeing him without favour. 'So you've shown up at last. Wondered when you were going to deign to put in an appearance.'

'Been busy.'

'Rather thought y'might be. How are things?'

'OK. I finished off that gastrectomy – patient's doing well.'

'Good.'

'Other patients going on much as expected. How are you?'

'Orrible. As y'can see for y'self. Daft, innit? *Me*, a bleeding coronary.'

'Common enough. Common enough to recover, too.'

'Yeah. Gonna concentrate on that. Leave you to look after the work.'

'Be good for me – and I reckon I ought to be able to manage by now. Anyway, Mummery's on the end of the telephone. Says I'm to ring him at any time, and he'll come up and consult at the drop of a hat. Coming up anyway next week, to do your outpatients and see patients in Harley Street too.'

As Nick had foreseen, Leo cheered up at the news, and his eyes, which had been sombre, danced evilly.

'That'll be great for you.'

'I haven't your expertise in handling him.'

'More than time y'learnt, then.'

'I dare say. Perhaps the girls'll be able to cope with him – they're working wonders in the office. All the paperwork seems to be tied up – Sophie's been down there helping Judith.' Nick expected this sort of trivial detail to be so relaxing as to be rated almost boring, and he was startled when Leo unmistakably twitched. Did he think Judith wasn't up to it? But then, Nick reminded himself, he'd specifically stated that Sophie was holding her hand. Whatever the cause, Leo was edgy. He must be tiring. Nick decided to get himself outside the room fast. 'Time I got down to the wards,' he said. 'I'll keep on looking in, though. But if there's anything you want, or anything that occurs to you I ought to have told you about, make them get me back up here stat, won't you? I'll come straight up – just tell sister to let me know, and I'll be here.'

'Will do,' Leo said. But his eyes were pre-occupied, and Nick went off cursing himself for having in some way mishandled the situation. He went along to sister's office further down the corridor to let her know what he'd told Leo about sending for him at any moment, and found James there with her, writing up notes. He looked up.

'What did you think of him?'

Nick sighed. 'Just as you said. A very sick man.' He frowned. 'I didn't think I was telling him anything worrying, but he was tired and a bit on edge when I left, so I cut my own visit short. I think I'll tell the department no one's to visit him yet. Be on the safe side. Do you agree?'

'The fewer the better, in my opinion, and certainly no one who might bother him, or start going into unnecessary detail about his patients. On no account must anyone bring him any problems requiring decisions. That's out.'

'I don't think they'd dream of it, but you can never be sure. Someone might think it was their duty to pass on every slight change, or check that what they were doing was precisely what he'd have done himself. Prevention is better than cure, so I'll lay it on the line, tell them all to keep away for the time being.'

James nodded. 'Sister, no visitors for Mr Rosenstein, other than Mr Waring here.'

'Very good, Mr Leyburn. I'll see that everyone knows.'

In fact, hardly had Nick and James departed than Stella arrived, calling in to see how Leo was before going on duty herself. Sister Barton was short with her. 'No visitors, Sister. Those were my instructions, only a few minutes ago, from Mr Leyburn, and I can't possibly make any exceptions.'

Stella hadn't, as it happened, expected to see Leo. She'd wanted only to hear how he was.

'Poorly, I'm afraid,' Sister Barton told her. 'And he's not to be troubled with work of any sort.'

'No, of course not.' Stella was slightly indignant. 'I wouldn't think of it. None of us would.' Did the cardiothoracic department imagine that everyone in general surgery was moronic?

As soon as she had gone, Sister Barton told her staff nurse about the no visitors ruling. 'I see now why Mr Leyburn was so firm about it. The theatre sister from general surgery has been up already. She said it was only to enquire, but if you ask me she'd have been in that cubicle in a flash if I hadn't stopped her.'

The staff nurse, who kept her ear closer to the ground than did Sister Barton, who thought about her job and very little else, had the explanation. 'Wasn't he supposed to have been having an affair with his theatre sister?'

'Oh, was he? That explains it, then. However, my instructions were quite clear. No visitors other than Mr Waring, that's what Mr Leyburn said, so put up a big notice on the door, and don't let a soul in without referring them to me first.'

The staff nurse hung a notice on Leo's door, and, in her coffee-break, related the story of Stella's attempt to see him. Since Leo was always food for hospital gossip – and more so now that he'd had a coronary practically in his own theatre – this new titbit was snapped up avidly, and went the rounds.

When Judith appeared, popping up to the cardiothoracic department in her lunch-hour, simply because she couldn't keep away even though she knew that Sophie, via Nick, would undoubtedly have the latest and most reliable information about Leo's progress, she got short shrift. Enquiring politely at sister's office, she was informed snappily by the staff nurse – Sister Barton was at lunch – that Mr Rosenstein was not to have any visitors. 'There's a notice on the door.'

Like Stella, Judith explained that she wanted only to hear how he was.

'Poorly.'

'Oh dear.'

'Lucky to be still with us. If it hadn't been for – did you say you were his secretary?'

'That's right.'

'You must be Judith Chasemore then.' The staff nurse looked her up and down with a very different eye. 'You gave him heart massage, didn't you? Is that right?'

'Well, he more or less dropped at my feet.'

'I can't alter the no visitors rule for you, sister would liquidate me.' The staff nurse was apologetic. 'But if you'd like to look through his window, I don't see why not.'

'Oh, I *would* like to.'

'Go ahead, then. But if you see sister coming back, evaporate stat, will you? Because if she finds out she'll slaughter me.'

'I'll keep out of her way. Don't worry. And thanks.' Uneasily Judith approached the cubicle. She longed to see Leo, yet at the same time she didn't know if she was going to be able to bear it.

She looked through the window.

He was asleep. He looked old and tired, and blue round the lips still. Her heart went out to him, and she longed to be able to slip into his room, take him into her arms and hold him until somehow, through the force of her love, he recovered.

Down the corridor, she glimpsed the dark blue of a senior sister's dress, and then she heard Sister Barton in conversation with Tom Rennison, the director of cardiothoracic surgery.

In fairness to the staff nurse, Judith turned and slipped out of the corridor and along towards the lift.

# Chapter 11

The news that Leo had had a coronary and been admitted to cardiothoracic intensive care spread fast, and telephone calls poured in to both Harley Street and the hospital from all over the country – and from overseas too. Northiam, who heard the news from James Leyburn, rang up from California, interrogating James as to Leo's progress and condition and proffering advice. Sophie pulled herself together, as she put it, and rang Melanie, who from then on telephoned regularly from New York, while any number of friends and former colleagues, from Michael Adversane to individuals who had once, years back, spent six months as Leo's house surgeon, enquired anxiously about his condition several times a week. Most of them suggested visiting him, and Nick and James came to the conclusion that it would be a good plan for Leo to see these outsiders, who could be relied on not to badger him about departmental detail – of which they knew nothing – but instead to entertain him by cheerful gossip from the past.

Nick, to everyone's enormous relief, was appointed a locum consultant to take over Leo's work for a month, while Jeremy Hillyard ran the department as senior registrar, and another registrar took his place and assisted Nick. Lord Mummery duly came up from the country and established himself in Harley Street, rather as if he'd never left. He marched in and out of

Leo's cubicle in intensive care exactly as he pleased –
much as he went in and out of the general theatre,
ostensibly ready to proffer advice but testing Nick's
nervous stamina severely. Michael Adversane came up
from the hospital on the coast where he and Jane were
working to persuade Leo to stay with them for his
convalescence. Lord Mummery made the same offer,
and Northiam, in another telephone call to James,
extended a similar invitation.

Leo turned them all down. 'Propose to convalesce in
me own flat, as soon as they allow me out of this rotten
little rabbit 'utch,' he said. 'Not goin' nowhere.'

This was not strictly accurate. He was nourishing a
secret dream. He and Judith would go to the house by
the river together.

He mentioned this plan to no one – nor did he
demand Judith's presence. He didn't want to see her.
He wasn't going, if he could help it, to let her set eyes
on him looking old and sick. He had, too, to make his
peace with his own conscience. Here he was, stuck in
intensive care after a coronary. He'd imagined, until
now, that he was going to look after Judith. The
position had been reversed, and he didn't know yet
what he was going to do.

He was already better, off oxygen and able to sit out
of bed in a chair, clad in various shades of silk Paisley
pyjamas, laundered daily by the faithful Mrs Noakes.
His heart, though, had so far failed to settle to James's
satisfaction. He and Tom Rennison, the director of
cardiothoracic surgery, and Amyas Miller, their
medical specialist, conferred over Leo regularly.
Superficially he seemed recovered, they agreed, yet his
tracing hadn't settled entirely, and his exercise
tolerance was nil.

'Worrying, that.'

'Give him time.'

'Carrying a good deal of extra weight, of course. That might account for it. Load on his circulation.'

'I've told him he'll have to go on a crash diet.'

'Yes. Six weeks off, and a crash diet, that's essential. After that with any luck he should be fine. After all, plenty of patients go on after a coronary to have twenty or more hardworking years. See no reason why he shouldn't be one of them.'

'In general surgery? Standing for hours, in the heat? Disturbed nights. Can we allow him to go back to that sort of existence? Isn't it asking for trouble?' Amyas Miller was one of the most cautious physicians in the hospital.

'We'll just have to see how he comes along. Early days yet. He must take it slowly.'

'What are we going to tell him, though, when he enquires about his future, as he's bound to – any day now, if you ask me.'

James Leyburn shook his head. 'Useless to try and keep the truth from him. He knows the score as well as we do.'

In fact, Leo didn't ask them the awkward question. He knew his own chances without being told.

Apart from James Leyburn and the cardiothoracic staff, he was hardly seeing anyone from inside the hospital other than, inevitably, Lord Mummery, and Nick, who had continued his earlier embargo on visits by Leo's staff. Nick had also instructed both Sophie and Judith to keep out of the way. Anything they needed to tell Leo could be transmitted by him, Nick said. He would be able to judge how fit Leo was each day.

With Lord Mummery making the Harley Street consulting-rooms his headquarters, and Aubrey

Everard and Nick seeing patients there too, Judith was run off her feet. She had no chance to repeat her lunch-hour visit to Leo.

The day they had spent together was slipping away into the past, and she almost began to wonder if it had ever taken place, or if she'd dreamt it. But on one point she was in no doubt whatever. She loved him.

But so, unfortunately, did others. Judith heard about Melanie's regular calls from New York, and Stella's visit to his cubicle, when Sister Barton had sent her packing. Sophie, too, wanted to go in and see him, but Nick continued his veto. Sophie argued.

'Honestly, Nick, surely you can trust me not to yatter away endlessly about work? I just want to see the sweet man.'

Judith decided to put her oar in – at what, unluckily, was quite the wrong moment – and proposed that she, too, might look in. 'Only for a couple of minutes.'

But this was too much. Towards Sophie alone Nick might easily have weakened. He turned them both down flat. 'Leave the poor bloke in peace, can't you? He'll manage to survive without seeing either of you for a week or two, and you'll have to learn to get along without him, the same as I do in the theatre. Nothing you need to ask him that Aubrey or I can't settle for you – or Lord Mummery, if it comes to that.' Neither he nor Sophie suspected that there might be any sort of special relationship between Leo and Judith. Stella, yes. But Judith – the idea didn't cross their minds.

Stella, as it happened, was the next to join the queue. In the theatre that same day, at the end of the list, she asked Nick if it would at last be possible for her to pay Leo a visit. 'Not, actually, about work,' she assured him, her brown eyes gleaming with an air of delighted mystery.

The theatre pinned its ears back.

Resigned, Nick gave in. After all, he explained later to an infuriated Sophie, it might do Leo a power of good at this stage to have a visit from one of his girlfriends.

Even if she wasn't the girl he was secretly yearning for, Leo was pleased to see Stella. She bounced into the little cubicle, straight from the theatre, still in uniform and obviously brimming with some sort of news.

'So what's 'appened?' he asked at once. 'You won the pools or something?'

'Just as good,' she assured him, her wide smile flashing. 'Trust you to ask, almost before I'm right in the room. No one else has spotted anything.'

'Siddown and tell y'r Uncle Leo.' He gestured at the chair by his bed, on which he was reclining ungracefully in pyjamas that, although they were a crescendo of orange and red swirls, failed entirely to drown his exuberance. He certainly looked neither old nor ill, though, unfortunately, he was unaware of this, nor was he any longer blue round the lips, Stella noted thankfully. 'I'm supposed to be restin' after what passes for a midday meal in this joint,' he told her. 'So shoot.'

'Tell me first how you are.'

He shrugged. 'Better than I was. Not as good as I'd like to be. The rest you can see with y'r own eyes. Sooner I get out of 'ere the better I'll be pleased, but they won't let me go yet. More tests. And I've got to be able to do two flights of stairs before they'll allow me 'ome to sleep in me own bed, rot them.'

'You gave us all one hell of a fright, Leo.'

'Gave meself one, too.'

'The theatre isn't the same without you,' she said, which was true enough. Then she recollected Nick's directive. She wasn't to talk about work, and if Leo asked her, she was to be sure to convince him they were managing splendidly. 'Not that we aren't getting on fine,' she added hastily. 'Nick's going great guns, and then, of course, we have Lord Mummery. Wow.'

'Yeah, I have him too.' Leo was laconic. 'He's OK. Don't understand why people make such a song and dance about 'im. I don't have no difficulty.'

'No.' Stella's wide smile gleamed again. 'Reckon you don't. But for us sinners he sure presents a problem.'

'Baloney. Anyway, I don't want to 'ear about 'im. Still waiting to be told y'r own news. You and Larry joined up again, that it?'

'So now you take the words out of my mouth,' she protested. Her eyes shone, and her mouth curved into radiance. 'That's it, anyway. You've got it.'

'Seems to suit you, anyway. Tell me from the beginning – what 'appened?'

'As a matter of fact, it all began the day you were struck down,' she said. 'I was feeling so miserable – all of us were frantically upset when you keeled over like that, and had to be carted off here.'

'Good,' he said. 'But go on. What 'appened?'

'Well, I was back in the flat, and feeling miserable, thinking about you up here and not knowing how you were, and the doorbell rang. I thought it might be Nick or someone with some news, and I went to answer it in a hurry – and there was Larry. First time he'd been since I moved in, but I forgot everything about all our rows and the way we'd parted, the things we'd both said, I just dragged him in and started telling him what had happened, I was so thankful to be able to talk to him about it.'

'And then?'

'And then, somehow or other, we both sort of just fell into each other's arms, and – and it was great. In fact, everything is on between us again, all stations go – has been from that moment.'

'Good,' he said shortly, wishing he could say the same for himself.

'It's fantastic to be together again.' Stella was oblivious of Leo, her eyes turned back to Larry and herself together in what had once been her lonely flat. 'He stayed with me that night, and – '

'That night and every night, I hope?' Leo gave her his glinting smile, and she never guessed at the moment of sadness and longing he'd put firmly behind him.

'Sure.' Filled with her own happiness, she took his hand. 'Thank you a million times,' she said, 'for seeing me through the period when we were apart, and giving such good advice. Telling me to hang on.'

'What are you both going to do now?' Leo asked, wondering if he'd have to tell Nick to start looking for a new theatre sister.

'He's decided to sell the house, would you believe? He's accepted a post as RSO at Tybalt's, so of course this means he'll be living in, and he says I can either live there with him or keep my own flat on and he'll spend his off-duty there.'

'That's it, then.' Leo was decided. 'That's the signal you were waiting for. If he gives up that house for you, you matter to him. No doubt of that. So stick to him, my girl, and when the day comes that you have to give up your post, retire into private life and be Mrs Laurence Bridge, housewife, for a few years, remember that it'll be your turn to do some giving up.'

He grinned, but his eyes challenged her.

Stella's brown eyes were liquid with love for Larry, but what bubbled over was affection for Leo – she wouldn't have dreamed of arguing with him, and his challenge passed her by entirely. 'I sure will remember,' she assured him, leaning forward and kissing him excitedly. 'Now I must go, I can see Sister Barton hovering outside the window – she'll be in any moment to throw me out So *au revoir*, and bless you for everything.'

Sister Barton had glanced through the window to make sure Stella wasn't wearing Leo out with theatre problems, but the eyeful that greeted her rocked her back on her neatly shod heels, and went round the hospital like a bushfire in a drought. Only one person from general surgery, apart from Nick Waring, had been to see Leo in intensive care, and that was his smashing theatre sister. They had held hands in his cubicle, and before leaving she had kissed him passionately.

No doubt now, the hospital decided, about Leo's affair with Stella. It was on. In fact, had it not been for the regular telephone calls from New York, they would have assumed a good deal more than a passing affair was under way. But with Melanie in the picture, they were left asking one another which of the beautiful couple the old womaniser was two-timing.

The story came at Judith from all quarters, greeted her on all sides, wherever she went. Her father was smiling quietly, and even Sophie and Nick were joking about it.

'The wicked old thing,' Sophie said affectionately. 'Here he is, at death's door – but with two females competing for him.'

Judith smiled a cool, reserved smile, presented a

calm front to the world, and reminded herself she hadn't really expected anything else. She'd known from the beginning that it was too good to be true that she should be Leo's latest regular date. Quite apart from the fact that he'd always been credited with any number of hectic affairs, she was a nobody, with a bad medical history, and years younger than he was. She was enormously lucky he'd gone so far as to make a few passes in her direction. She'd treasure the memory. A day and two nights.

She hoped, gritting her teeth with resolution, that he'd recover comepetely from his coronary and live on to experience long years of happiness with Stella or any lovely actress with whom he finally decided to settle down. The main object was that he should live to a ripe old age, and she found she was praying fervently for him to go on living. Just that.

She should have had more faith in him. Even immured in intensive care, he remained more than capable of organising his own life to his own satisfaction, and in the intervals of chatting to the streams of visitors who poured in and out he'd been doing a lot of quiet unobtrusive thinking. He missed Judith, but he wasn't going to say anything to anyone until he had everything sorted out in his own mind.

It was not Judith's bad prognosis that made him pause now, but his own. Now that he'd turned out to be a bad risk, ought he to drop all his plans for spending the rest of his life with her?

For the first few days after his coronary, he was ready for the great sacrifice. He had to abandon all claim to that lovely tawny-haired Judith of his, who, in any case, would be bound to lose interest in an old man with a wonky heart and a tired look.

Long hours in intensive care accompanied by some

hard thinking soon convinced him, however, that such an attitude, while poignantly dramatic, had little to do with reality. What if he was no longer such a good prospect as a husband? He loved her, and if he did happen to die before the year was out, he'd have done her no harm by marrying her. Even a bit of good, maybe. She'd be well provided for. With his funds behind her, if her health should go downhill and he not be around to look after her, she'd have access to the best possible care and treatment. If he died, she'd be a rich young woman.

He grinned to himself. More bloody drama. He wasn't going to die. Not if he could help it. Even though there was that uncomfortable memory of his father's death nagging away at him. His father had had a heart attack in middle age, exactly as he'd now done himself, and it had killed him off. But that, after all, had been almost twenty years ago, when much less had been known about heart disease. Today, open-heart surgery had become almost routine, for anyone who needed it. Not that he was going to need surgery himself. A strict diet, regular exercise and a bit of a rest should be enough to rehabilitate him, even though James might pull a long face and hint at the possibility of surgery at some unspecified date in the future.

Well, whatever happened, he'd see that everything was lined up so that Judith was looked after. With that settled, he felt easier in his mind than he'd done for months, and drifted off into a dreamless sleep.

He was astonished, and a bit annoyed, to be awoken in the dawn hours to find James leaning over him with a serious face, his registrar and house surgeon hovering and fiddling about, a night sister there too, and a rapid patter of feet coming and going.

James went over him as thoroughly as if he'd been a new emergency admission.

Leo knew better than to interrupt them. They had a reason. No one would have fetched James over to him from his bed at home if it hadn't been essential.

'So what's all this in aid of?' he demanded, as soon as they were through.

James nodded to his registrar and houseman, and they slipped out of the cubicle with the night sister and a staff nurse. James sat down comfortably in the chair at the bedside, looking more than ever like some easy-going farmer from the deep country, his big hands planted squarely on his knees, his kindly face more placid than usual.

'Going to be a bit of a facer, Leo. I'm sorry. But you seem to have had a silent coronary during the night. The monitors showed it up.'

'Hell.' He stared at James. 'Wasn't aware of nothing.'

'No. That's all to the good, then. Well, we'll just have to watch it and see how you go. Take it easy today, I think, don't you? Don't get up. Not until I've seen you again, anyway. And I think we'll stop all visitors – for twenty-four hours at least. All right?'

'Have to be. You're the judge.'

'Lie back. Do nothing. Think tranquil thoughts. I'll look in again before my round.'

He went out of the room, and Leo indulged in a bout of fluent and very basic swearing.

The young night sister came back. 'Mr Leyburn has written this up for you, Mr Rosenstein.'

Leo glared at her. 'Take it away. Not havin' it. Some bloody tranquilliser, I've no doubt. Tell him –' he broke off. Judith. He was going to live on and marry Judith. To bring that about, he'd swallow any damned pills they shoved at him. 'All right. Give it here.'

He had a very quiet day, sleeping a good deal of the time. When he wasn't dozing – and often when he was – he thought about Judith.

# Chapter 12

The next morning Leo telephoned his solicitor, and
informed Sister Barton she was to let him in without
delay when he arrived. 'Goin' to make me will.'

Sister Barton was horrified, and the next Leo knew
not the solicitor but James appeared in his cubicle.
She'd sent for him.

'What's all this I hear about a solicitor and your will,
Leo? There's really no occasion for you to take such a
despairing view.'

'Not a despairing view at all.' The dark eyes glinted
triumphantly. 'Gonna get married.'

James's eyes widened. So he's going to marry that
theatre sister of his, he thought. What a turn-up for
the books. What about Melanie, ringing up from New
York several times a week? The words almost popped
out of his mouth, but he swallowed them.

'Then I want to see Judith Chasemore,' Leo said.
'I'll tell Nick to send her along. You tell sister she's to
allow her in.'

This was going too far. 'You're not to do any work.'
James was decisive. 'Get married if you must, but I'm
not having your secretary in here and you dictating
letters. No way.'

'Not going to dictate to her. Going to propose.'

This was the knock-out, and sent James reeling.

Leo surveyed him with considerable amusement,
not to mention self-satisfaction. 'Surprised you, has

it?' He nodded. 'Crafty, that's me. People often don't know what I'm up to until I've been and gone and done it.' He sat smugly in bed with ECG monitors stuck all over his hairy chest, and nodded again. 'Allow me to see me future wife, if you don't mind, before you start practising y'r hideous trade on me – take it you're set on a new battery of tests? And I suppose I'm in for cardiac catheterisation? Never thought I'd come to that.'

'Who'd have thought you'd have come to the point of proposing to any girl?' James retorted, recovering his nerve. 'Sure you're all right?'

'Perfectly clear in me head, if that's what you mean. Thought it all out careful-like. Reached a firm decision. But I'm quite calm in me mind, and I understand me own limitations. Me present limitations, that is. Don't want to see her until tomorrow. Fix things up with the solicitor today, see her tomorrow.'

'What about getting all steamed up when she's here? Don't think I approve of that.'

'Lusting after women 'as never done me no 'arm. The uncertainty may 'ave panicked me a bit, but I intend to live to marry the girl.'

'Uncertainty over now, Leo?' James was very gentle. 'Sure?'

'Quite sure. Not to worry. 'Ad some notion earlier that because I was a bad risk, it became me duty to give 'er up. Load of nonsense. Anyway, you're not gonna let me die, are you?'

'Not if I can have a bit of co-operation from you. How about conforming to some good co-operative patient behaviour as from now, eh? Take your nice tablets from the kind doctor.' He beckoned to Sister Barton, hovering outside the window in her accustomed manner. 'Mr Rosenstein will have those tablets now, Sister.'

Leo growled, but he took the tablets and swallowed them, and the following morning he agreed also, to James's surprise, to accept the tranquilliser he prescribed, before Judith came to visit him.

'I intend to preserve your miserable life, in spite of your efforts to the contrary,' James told him.

Judith could be seen outside the window, looking anxious, and accompanied by Sister Barton, wearing a reproving expression and talking urgently.

'No, I know, Sister,' she was saying. 'I'm not going to say a word about work, or even answer any questions. I've been talking to Mr Waring, and I promised him I wouldn't utter.'

Nick and Sophie had both been distictly odd about her visit to Leo. First of all, there'd been the horrifying news of his second coronary – news which had shattered not only Judith, but most of them in general surgery – and then, before she'd properly recovered from that, Nick told her she could go and see Leo. He'd been asking for her, and James Leyburn had agreed she should go in that morning.

Judith began to wonder what she ought to take with her.

'You're not to mention work at all.' Nick was firm.

'No, I won't. But what shall I say if he brings it up?'

'Just play it by ear, duckie, and tell him I'll scalp you if you come out with a single note.' Nick was unperturbed about Leo dictating letters to Judith, since James Leyburn had told him why Leo wanted to see her. He'd been as staggered as James, and a good deal more put out.

'Is he out of his mind or something? *Judith*? Marry her? But there's Stella, and that actress in New York.

They both think – '

'That they're his girlfriends. I know. But neither of them, I'd hazard a guess, expects to marry the old devil.'

'No. No, I'm pretty sure they don't. But they don't expect him to up and marry anyone else, either.'

'Then they're in for a surprise.'

Nick had gone straight home and told Sophie, who had been enthusiastic. 'It might turn out to be terrific for both of them,' she assured Nick. 'So let's send Judith along to see him, and keep our fingers crossed.'

Hardly surprising, though, that Judith found their attitude perplexing. Sophie was blind to queries about tricky letters or postponed appointments, and even the newly arrived proofs of the article for the *Quarterly Review* – which Judith had planned to take in as pleasant light reading for the patient – left her cold. She seemed only interested in what Judith was going to wear.

'Wear? This, I suppose. Why not?'

'You don't think you might rush home and put on something a bit – a bit – well, more exciting than those old jeans?'

'Leo's not going to notice what I'm wearing,' Judith said snappily. Inwardly she was in tears. The green tracksuit had come unbidden into her mind, and the green beads she hadn't allowed him to buy. Emeralds, he'd wanted to get, that day. Everything had been filled with promise, and it had all been snatched away, before she'd so much as had a chance to let him know what it had meant to her.

Sophie could easily have screamed. 'I think you should go home this instant and put on that copper suede outfit you wear sometimes. It really does things for you.'

The cool grey eyes looked blank. 'You must be joking,' Judith said. 'Leo wouldn't expect me to dress up.' And off she went, to Sophie's irritation, in her shabby jeans with a blue checked shirt and an ancient navy sweater, to hover irresolutely outside the flower shop in Great St Anne's. Leo would think her demented if she went in with a sheaf of gladioli, and you couldn't take someone like him a tiny posy of violets or freesias. Her lips quirked. It was the first time she'd genuinely felt like smiling for days – yet nothing was any better. Worse, really. But an extraordinary change seemed to be occurring within her. Anxiety and depression were fading away, excitement and an upsurge of gaiety were rising. The prospect of spending a mere ten minutes with Leo in his cubicle in intensive care was making her eyes dance and her heart sing. In the old days she would have skipped along the pavements. Now she couldn't risk a stumble, but trod carefully, erect and steadily, holding a dozen red roses and feeling a bit of a fool, but far too excited to care.

She went up in the lift, through the heavy doors that hissed open as she approached, and along the busy corridor – which might, as far as she was concerned, have been empty – and into Leo's cubicle. A tall slender girl in shabby jeans, her grey eyes alive and her roses glowing brilliantly.

Leo saw her appear in the big window at the end of his bed, and knew he'd love her for ever. There she was. His girl.

He didn't, as it happened, even notice the roses she was clasping a little feverishly. All he saw was her tawny hair shining like a beacon of joy.

And then it all fell apart.

She gave him the roses, in an off-hand, embarrassed

fashion, and he, taken by surprise, failed to hold on to her hand and was left clutching his flowers.

He had never proposed to anyone before. Not he. Not likely. And now this practised womaniser found himself at a loss. He opened his mouth. No words came. He shut it, swallowed, gave himself a mental shake, cursed James's tranquilliser which must be slowing him up exactly when he needed all his wits, and tried again, announcing fiercely that he wanted to talk to her. Seriously. 'Siddown.'

Judith sat gingerly on the edge of the visitors chair.

'Nearer than that.'

Judith hitched the chair a nervous two inches towards the high hospital bed.

Leo gave up. 'We oughta get married,' he said angrily.

Judith's heart gave a great leap of joy, and then her stomach opened and received her leaping heart. Blank despair invaded her.

'Why?' she asked him frigidly, sure she already knew the answer.

'*Why*?' He eyed her furiously. If only he'd let the words fall out of his mouth the situation could have been retrieved. But instead of saying 'because I love you,' he remarked, as coldly as she had spoken, 'be a good plan, wouldn't you say?'

This underlined Judith's fear.

Leo thought he was going to die. And before he died, he was going to see she was looked after. He thought that one day she was going to be really ill and disabled, unable to support herself, so he was going to see to it she had money – after he was dead. There'd be a pension from the health service for his widow, and the Rosenstein trust funds too. Everyone knew Leo had no need to work, he could live on his investments alone, even without the greengrocery chain. So now, believing he wasn't going to survive, he was going to see she had all this cash behind her.

Judith's dream was quite other. What she wanted was to look after Leo, and she certainly didn't see herself as his pensioner. Aching with desolation, for already the conviction that if he thought he was dying he was almost bound to be right had taken possession of her, she looked at him with her grey eyes wide with pain.

This had been Leo's first proposal, and it was likely to be his last, too, he decided, if it made his love look at him with her normally cool eyes blazing with agony. Plainly the idea of marrying him turned her right off. He'd made some sort of mistake.

Judith, filled with determination, pushed her fear away. Leo was going to live. She personally would force him into living, if it came to it. No way was she going to entertain for two minutes this notion that he was dying. He was going to live. That was how she was going to look at it, whatever it cost her.

'We can talk about it when you're convalescent,' she informed him in a brittle, anguished little voice. 'After you're out of here.'

It seemed he'd proposed and been turned down. 'All right.' He was cross. 'Thanks for the flowers, anyway. They're nice.'

'Oh, I don't know.' She was floundering. 'Silly of me, really, I suppose.'

'No, I like them.' What was happening? Why hadn't he grabbed her the moment she came in and – and what? Made love to her? In intensive care, strung up to half a dozen monitors and with Sister Barton peering in at the window? Stinking hospital.

They were both almost relieved to see the professor

of medicine come in.

'James asked me to look in and rùn the rule over you, in view of this question of surgery,' he announced.

'I'll go,' Judith said hastily, and made for the door.

Leo clutched at his remaining wits. 'No,' he snapped. 'I mean yes. OK. But wait. Come back. Wanna talk.' By now he was bellowing in the direction of Judith's inexorably retreating back.

# Chapter 13

Judith stared out of the window across roofs and buildings familiar from childhood. This morning, though, they looked entirely different from ever before, seemed to carry an edge of excitement, were transfigured by a quality of luminous promise, etched as brilliantly as though a master painter, in a moment of earth-shattering revelation, had illuminated them especially for her.

She drew a deep breath.

Leo had proposed to her. He'd suggested they should marry.

They'd spend the rest of their lives, long or short, together. They'd have, unbelievably, claims on each other.

A small depressed voice from somewhere inside her, quite out of tune with the uproar in the rest of her body, reminded her of the unwelcome truth as she'd seen it only minutes earlier. 'Only because he's sorry for you. Because he thinks he's going to die, and he wants to see you all right first. Nothing more.'

But these demoralising views, which had so shaken her in Leo's presence, had lost their sting. What did it matter what his motivation was? He'd handed her heaven on a plate, and she was not handing it back. Not likely. Instead, she'd grab this incredible opportunity with both hands. What if she did have to sit around watching him wonder why he'd ever

married her? She'd face that problem when it arose –
and if it arose. What about Stella, or Melanie in New
York? One day either of them – or someone still
unknown – might take him from her. Someone would
come along, and she'd see his eyes turn towards the
new arrival, and recognise he loved her. She'd be filled
with that same aching pain she'd experienced five
minutes earlier in his cubicle.

But by then she'd have had some sort of life with
him. To lose him would be unbelievable agony, yet not
to take the joy he was offering now was unthinkable.
She was going to step straight into that cubicle, the
instant the professor of medicine came out, before
anyone else had a chance to slip in, and she was going
to accept his proposal. She'd be mad if she didn't.
Accept and to hell with the consequences. Take
whatever pain it brought with it. She was going to be
engaged to Leo Rosenstein.

The world shifted into incandescent glory. Judith
turned round from the window and stared obsessively
at Leo's door, ready to hurl herself back inside, and
grab him and his offer.

The professor came out. Jet-propelled, Judith
hurtled in.

Leo took one look at her, opened his arms and took
her confidently into them. His mouth found hers, and
Judith kissed him back adoringly, opening her mouth
to his, putting her own arms round him to press them
still closer together. They were far too happy to talk.
Leo knew he didn't need to repeat his proposal, which
had come off, after all. This was his girl. He'd been, as
he first supposed, one hundred per cent right. Judith
didn't even need to tell him – though later she did try
to explain – why she'd apparently changed her mind.
He knew, as if he'd been out there in the corridor with

her, what she'd felt, why she'd come back.

She'd come back because she loved him. Judith was for him. What was more, he was going to live through this minor interruption to his wellbeing, this small coronary episode, he was going out of this cubicle on his two feet, to take Judith back to his flat, and make furious love to her. For days on end.

He felt terrific. It was like being a boy again and in love with Jane, only this time round he was no uncertain boy, but a confident man. This time round it was all going to happen.

No one was going to walk off with his girl under his nose, as Mike Adversane had done with Jane.

'Jude,' he said, suddenly coming up for air. 'Ring the Adversanes and get them both up here.'

'The Adversanes?' Leo's friends, living down on the coast somewhere.

'Yeah. Telephone number's in the book.'

'When do you want them to come up?'

'For our wedding. Witnesses.'

'Our wedding?' It was an inelegant squawk.

'Going to marry me, aren't you?'

'Oh, yes.' She snuggled cosily back into his arms.

'Well, then, sooner the better, eh? Get organised. Get a special licence, and we can be married in the hospital. Sophie will see to it – you get straight on to her and get it laid on between you.'

'But –'

'Do want to, don't you?'

'Oh, yes, Leo.'

'In that case, I can see no cause for delay.'

'People will –'

'People nothing. They can get lost. You and I are the only ones who matter, and it's what we want that decides anything. So get cracking. Better choose a

ring, too. Get on the blower to Izzy – he's bin looking
out some emeralds.'

Judith gaped at him. '*Emeralds*?'

'Yeah. Choose one – dare say Sophie'll go with you,
if you ask her. And don't be mean on account of it's
my money you're going to be spending. Ring of a
lifetime – right?'

'Right.'

'He'll have some sort of chain, too, for you. Oh, and
you'd better choose a wedding ring while you're at it.
Take the lot, and tell 'im to send the bill to me.'

There was no withstanding him in this mood, and
in any case Judith had no desire to hold up either their
marriage or anything that Leo thought should go with
it, such as rings, a wedding dress, the champagne he
told her to order, or the food she was to instruct Mrs
Noakes to lay in.

She had to encounter opposition. Rob Chasemore
took some convincing that the marriage was going to
be successful, and since he was too good a physician to
argue about it with Leo in intensive care, Judith had
to sit up late at nights talking him round.

Her mother, too, was difficult to satisfy. She hated
both the rushed wedding and the fact that her
daughter's future would be tied to Leo's, whom she
remembered in his younger and more disreputable
days. Luckily for Judith, transatlantic telephone calls
were not cheap, and there was a limit to what could be
said in a few minutes. What she wasn't able to say
followed by airmail, but Judith was far too pressed for
time to bother to decipher the closely written pages.
She had more important problems on her hands. Leo
was to undergo surgery.

After the second coronary, he had another mass of
tests and investigations, and once the results were

through, James came along to his cubicle, with an assortment of notes and sketches, and an envelope of films.

'What've you got there?' Leo demanded at once. 'Are those mine?'

'Yes. These are the angio shots we took yesterday.' He wagged the envelope under Leo's twitching nose.

'What do they show?'

James pulled up a viewing box to the bedside. 'Have a look.'

Both of them scrutinised the films, and finally James said 'No doubt, it seems to me, we can spot the cause of your symptoms here.' He pointed with a battered ballpoint. 'Good news, I'd say, because it means its remediable.'

'Blow me, it's a Northiam's anomaly, isn't it?'

'That's it.' James nodded. 'Glad you agree.'

'Imagine me having that – what a turn-up for the books. Must've had it all me life, too – the one in a thousand conditions that looks and behaves like a coronary, but isn't. Reckon that's what me Dad must've had. Only they didn't pick it up then – Northiam wasn't around in time for him.' Leo didn't James to spell out to him the fact that his arteries were not, after all, diseased. He sighed with relief, and grinned cheerfully at James.

'We can put this right, using Northiam's new technique, and you'll be fit as a flea. Better than you were before, in fact, because you'll no longer have this underlying condition, waiting to play you up.'

'Great, isn't it? When can we get it done?'

'When depends on who does it, and where.'

'Here, of course. Where else? I've bin a Central man all me days – you don't suppose I'm gonna take off for some place else at this juncture?'

'There's the Ocean Hospital, and Northiam, with all his experience,' James pointed out.

'You do it, mate. What've you been out at the Ocean Hospital for, all those weeks while I was belting round the States, if not to bring yourself thoroughly up to date with exactly the surgery I need?'

'Of course we could do it here, there's no doubt of that. Or you could go out to California. Both Northiam and I would be delighted to do it – I spoke to him on the telephone half an hour ago – it's up to you.'

Leo didn't hesitate. 'I'd feel happier here at the Central, in your hands.'

'Thank you, Leo.' It had been a big compliment, though in no way undeserved. 'I'll be glad to do it for you. And I must say I'm immensely relieved it turns out after all to be something we can put right. Your heart muscle doesn't seem to be damaged, either, so we needn't delay, we can go more or less straight ahead with the corrective procedure. How would you feel about next Wednesday, if we can arrange it?'

'The sooner the better. Then I'll be out of here and on me honeymoon.'

On this occasion James let the remark pass, but a day or two later he put forward a firm recommendation that Leo should postpone his wedding until after his operation.

Leo would have none of it. 'If anything has to be postponed, it won't be the wedding,' he said.

James didn't pursue the argument. He and Rob Chasemore, while united in wishing the wedding could be delayed, were agreed that they hadn't a hope of persuading Leo or Judith to give in.

'And after all, happiness has never yet harmed any patient, as far as I know,' James said. 'So although a wedding may not be exactly the tranquilliser I'd have chosen for him, he's got one huge advantage. He's in love, and he's set on staying alive. So I dare say he'll be reasonably sensible.'

'I wish I could say the same of Judith. She seems possessed by fanatical energy – I can't get her to slow down.'

'This entire situation is hard on her.'

'It is. And I've had to point out to her that any major operation, and this is open-heart surgery with pulmonary by-pass, constitutes a risk. She has to be prepared for that.'

Lord Mummery, however, was in favour of the wedding. He'd taken to Judith, and wanted nothing more than to see her married to Leo, and the sooner the better.

He marched into Leo's cubicle to inform him of this, afterwards embarking on a long harangue, the gist of which was that Leo should take a good long period of convalescence. 'Go on a cruise. Opt out from this place for a while. Enjoy your lovely wife, eh, m'boy?'

'Have every intention of doing so.'

'Good. Excellent. Well, y'know y'can both come to us in Hereford, and I've heard you y'can also go to the Adversanes down on the coast. I've no doubt half a dozen others would like to have you. Or, as I say, a cruise.'

'I've got plans – '

'Y'have? Splendid. What are they?'

Leo had not had any notion of imparting them to Lord Mummery, of all people. However, not for the first time, he found himself overruled by his old chief, who extracted from his unwilling lips the full details of a proposal he'd planned to share only with Judith. 'I've got this little 'ouse,' he heard himself beginning.

'Down by the river. I rather thought we might go there for a while.'

'Do that. Need any help with the arrangements? Is it in running order?'

For a short wild moment Leo thought Lord Mummery was about to offer to hoover the place, or stock the refrigerator, and put hot-water bottles in the bed.

The next sentence disabused him of this idea. 'No matter.' Lord Mummery waved any reply away, as he had been in the habit of doing on ward rounds when a student's answer proved too tedious. 'No matter. Anything needs doing, I've no doubt the Warings between them can see to it. Anything you'd like me to tell them?'

Delegate, delegate. Always delegate. Leo remembered Lord Mummery's frequent injunction. 'Keep your own energy and skill for what no one but you can do. Let the rest of them get on with everything else.'

In a surprisingly mild voice, Leo said he thought Judith was seeing to everything.

Lord Mummery nodded approvingly. 'Delightful girl. A treasure. You've chosen well, m'boy.'

Leo, to his own consternation, went pink with pleasure.

Lord Mummery observed him closely, and remarked benignly 'Doesn't seem to be much wrong with y'r circulation, I'd say. Dare say ye'll live to make old bones.' Leaving this encouraging phrase behind him, he departed, off to plague Nick in the general surgery theatre.

The next day Judith's mother Daphne flew in. She greeted Rob in a friendly but distinctly absent-minded fashion, and demanded to know where her daughter was.

'Oh, rushing about somewhere,' Rob said uneasily. 'I've hardly seen her for days. She's moved her things over to Leo's flat, and she's sleeping there now.'

'This wedding simply ought not to be taking place.' Daphne was angry and frustrated. 'It's unsuitable in every way.'

'No good telling me,' Rob said. 'You can try telling Judy, but you may as well save your breath. She won't listen.'

Daphne snorted. 'As soon as that girl sets foot in this flat, I shall tell her what I think about it. What about her own health?'

'She's a good deal better.'

Daphne sighed impatiently. 'I suppose that's something. Anyway, Rob, how can they get married tomorrow? It's been so quick. Is it legal?'

He nodded. 'Judith, under Leo's direction, seems to have fixed it. A special licence, and the hospital chaplain.'

'But Leo surely can't be Church of England.'

'He doesn't seem bothered about that, and nor is the chaplain, apparently. Nor the Archbishop, who's duly disgorged the licence.'

Daphne, who was a good-looking, poised and well-groomed lady of forty-five, gobbled like a turkey. Her voice rose stridently, and to Rob she looked and sounded exactly as she had done in the days when they had both been medical students and she'd begun to harangue him about the injustices of the Central's medical school. He began to relax. She hadn't changed. This was familiar stuff. Once he'd been used to it – thank God he no longer was. Suddenly his present single existence was a precious possession, and he knew clearly why they'd separated.

'Don't pester the girl,' he said. 'I've done my best to put both sides to her. But she loves Leo – there's no doubt of that – and he wants to marry her. There are advantages as well as disadvantages, and she's under considerable pressure. Don't add to it.'

He might, however, have been talking to himself, and he had a hard evening, as when Judith failed to put in an appearance, Daphne transferred her superabundant energies to reorganising the flat for him, and planning a new dietary régime with the housekeeper, based on the latest American research.

In the morning, while they were at breakfast, Judith rang through from Leo's flat. Daphne swallowed her toast and peanut butter and rushed over to see her. Rob, fearing female recriminations, refused to join her, saying he had to go over to general surgery and do a round before the wedding at midday.

He need not have worried. Judith was much more expert at dealing with Daphne than Rob had ever been – in fact, she and her mother understood one another very well – and she was soon able to convince her that she loved Leo, he loved her, that in spite of both their health problems they were going to be married that morning. She must forget her anxiety, and come to the ceremony 'trying to look as if you're pleased'.

'All right, darling.' Daphne's resistance collapsed. 'I'm sorry if I've seemed unenthusiastic. But it was a shock to know you're going to be married to a man awaiting surgery in intensive care – even if it does happen to be Leo Rosenstein.' She looked her daughter up and down, and added, 'But if he can make you look like this, it must be all right.' Usually justifiably satisfied with her own appearance as a sophisticated career lady, Daphne all at once felt middle-aged and dowdy, while her hair, that she'd been so sure was keeping its colour for ever, beside Judith's shining head looked lifeless and gingery. 'What are you going to wear?' she asked, pushing her preoccupations firmly aside and turning herself resourcefully into a traditional mother of the bride, even if it was at the eleventh hour.

Judith waved a casual hand at the creamy embroidered caftan, at last coming into its own, and at the tiara beside it.

Daphne caught her breath. 'Don't tell me Leo bought that for you. I can't believe it.'

Judith shook her head. 'He doesn't even know about it. It was his friend Izzy. He rang and asked me about a headdress, and I had to say I hadn't anything. So he insisted on coming round to look at the caftan, and went off mysteriously. And last night he waltzed in with that. It's on loan, he says, and it's insured, and he's collecting it again tonight. Isn't it fantastic?'

'Beautiful.'

Wearing Izzy's tiara and her caftan Judith made a bride to draw all eyes when she and Leo were married by the hospital chaplain in the cubicle in intensive care.

Afterwards there was champagne for everyone, but the guests, under James's orders, drank a quick toast to bride and groom and slipped out into the corridor, where they made a lot of noise and toasted Sister Barton. Only Leo and Judith were left in his cubicle, drinking to one another and holding hands in what Sophie and Nick, monitoring proceedings through the window, agreed was a very sweet and touching manner.

'I think it's going to work,' Nick said. 'It certainly seems to have done them both a power of good so far.'

In the cubicle, Leo and Judith went into a clinch.

'Wow,' Nick said. 'Watch that.'

'Attagirl.' Sophie was admiring.

Within the cubicle, though, they were oblivious of the onlookers.

At last Leo said 'Right, off y'go. Gotta look after y'r wedding guests now.'

'I can stay another minute or two.'

'No, y'cant. Lord Mummery's out there, remember? Not to mention half the hospital'll be showing up at the flat over the lunch-hour, expecting to find some sort of celebration. So cut along and feed the mob.'

Judith looked mutinous.

'Go on. If y'don't, James'll be in and throw you out.'

'Oh, all right.' She kissed him again, and then turned to leave, the flowers Sophie had bought her in her hand, her head high.

'Y'tarara's crooked,' Leo warned, his fruity voice thick with laughter. 'Muggins,' he added tenderly.

Judith turned her head and winked at him, straightened the tiara, and swept grandly out of the cubicle and into the crowded corridor.

Lord Mummery, who knew his position in the order of precedence as well as – or, to be truthful, a good deal better than – anyone else, fielded her neatly. 'Allow me, my dear,' he said, 'to stand in for that husband of yours and escort you over to the flat.'

'Thank you,' Judith said. She'd grown used to him in these weeks while he'd been consulting in Harley Street, and the first shock the assembled company received from the new Mrs Leo Rosenstein was her ability to handle the Central's most irascible lord not only with aplomb but apparently with an almost daughterly affection. 'How sweet of you.' She took his arm, he patted her hand. Her parents materialised, and he addressed them rather as if they had been junior students. 'just follow me and the bride, and we'll lead you over to that nice flat of Leo and Judith's, where I've no doubt we'll find a spread. Eh?'

'That's right,' Judith agreed. 'And everybody's invited.'

'Come along then, all of you.'

Daphne and Rob Chasemore, correct and immaculately garbed, but distinctly bemused, fell in obediently behind Lord Mummery and their radiant daughter.

Halfway along the corridor Judith stopped abruptly. 'Sister Barton, I know M – ' she had been about to say Mr Rosenstein, but managed to bite the words back. 'I know my husband would want you to come over to the flat and drink our health there, as well as out in the passage here. Can you spare a moment?'

Sister Barton would be delighted to spare a moment.

'And that nice staff nurse, too. In fact any of you who can get away – it'll be quite all right to take it in turns. General surgery are standing in for one another, and coming over almost on a rota, so please appear exactly when it suits you and you can find a moment.' She smiled hugely. 'Lord Mummery and I will be expecting you.'

'Quite right, my dear.' He patted her hand again approvingly.

The assembled wedding guests were almost as overwhelmed by Lord Mummery's unaccustomed amiability as by Judith Chasemore's sudden metamorphosis into Mrs Rosenstein.

The flat was full of flowers, and Mrs Noakes was putting the finishing touches to the food Judith and Sophie had spent the previous evening preparing. Champagne flowed – poured copiously by Nick and Jeremy Hillyard – food circulated almost non-stop, and Central gossip was bandied about avidly.

James Leyburn arrived, carrying a large brown envelope, and made for Judith. 'Your husband is sitting back and drinking tea,' he said. 'So I told him I'd come over here and have some champagne with you – and I've this for your mother. Is she still here?'

'Over there.' Judith pointed.

'Good. Because I've a set of Leo's films and ECGs, together with my notes and a sketch or two, that I want her to take back to Northiam. No harm in a second opinion.'

# Chapter 14

Judith woke in Leo's bed, in what she still thought of as his flat, and by the hollow clutch at her stomach that grabbed her almost before she opened her eyes, she knew that the day ahead was frightening.

The day of the operation.

No good lying in bed being miserable. She looked at her bedside clock – her own clock, that she'd brought with her. Would there be a future in which her own and Leo'd possessions amalgamated, became part of their flat? When they bought curtains or carpets together for their home? Or would the worst happen, and Leo never return here?

She swung her legs down the side of the bed, reached for her housecoat, dragged it on, went to the bathroom and showered. If thoughts like these were all she could find, breakfast and out, fast.

Breakfast, though, proved another ordeal, recalling, as it immediately did, those days of unthinking happiness when she'd come back here after swimming with Leo, imagining all life to be ahead of them both.

Hell, so it was.

Open-heart surgery was nothing these days, as James repeated daily. 'It just takes a long time, that's all. Not to worry, Judith. Your old man is going to come through, and end up fitter than before.'

If only she dared believe him. But statistics weren't always wrong, and they said there was a high risk.

And this would be the first time this operation had been carried out by anyone but Northiam, the first time, too, it had been done in the Central – or in this country at all. No one, either, would suggest that to have your circulation taken over by a machine while surgeons fiddled about behind your heart was a nothing.

Leo would have had his pre-medication by now. She drank her coffee strong and scalding. The telephone rang.

She rushed to it. Leo had had another attack, he had collapsed in the night, he was lying there now, not pre-medicated but already dead, before the operation that would have saved him, had it been in time.

Sophie. 'How are you? Just thought I'd give you a ring in case you were on your own and feeling awful.'

Judith sighed. 'Yes, to both those things.'

'Oh, Jude, I am so sorry.'

Judith could have wept at the hideous name. 'Oh, Soph,' she said. 'I don't how I'm going to last out the day.'

'Shall I come over?'

'No, don't bother. I haven't long really. Lord Mummery is picking me up at nine.'

'Well, I just hope you feel up to him, that's all. He means well, I know.'

'He's being so incredibly kind, but – '

'But it's a bit of a strain, being on the receiving end of Mummery's kindness. I know. Nearly as bad as when he's in a rage. Nick is getting thinner daily, having him around here and in the department too. He thinks he's holding the place together, of course – and I must say, he does lend tone. No one dares push Nick around – only Mummery himself, that is.'

'He's awful, but I am rather fond of him,' Judith

said faintly. 'He – he holds my hand, you know. And I like it.'

'What,' Sophie asked methodically, 'are you going to wear, Jude?'

'Wear?' Judith was startled.

Sophie sighed. Just as she'd supposed. Judith hadn't given her clothes a thought. '*Wear*,' she repeated. 'Put on, dress in. What creation do you propose to don for the occasion?'

'What I wear is the last thing –'

'No, it isn't. Look, you can't totter in to the hospital for Leo's open-heart surgery on Lord Mummery's arm in a pair of jeans and a fisherman's sweater.'

'I suppose I can't.' Judith sounded as surprised as she felt.

Sophie sighed again, heavily this time, so that it floated down the line and Judith heard, as Sophie meant her to. 'Pull yourself together and think. A lot of people are going to stare at you – well, they'd stare at anyone with Mummery – but they're going to say to each other "so that's Leo Rosenstein's new wife." '

Judith felt an entirely different sort of clutch at her stomach, and cast wildly round in her mind for a suitable garment. The green tracksuit that Leo liked so much would hardly do for partnering Lord Mummery. One or two restaurant dresses – no, they'd be wrong, too.

'Neat but not gaudy,' Sophie said unhelpfully. 'On the other hand, something to do credit to Leo and awful Lord M.'

Judith groaned. 'Hell,' she said. 'I haven't a clue.'

'Then I'll come over,' Sophie announced. 'With you in about five minutes. Nick'll drop me off on his way in.' She put the telephone down, and nodded across the breakfast table at her husband. 'She was miserable as sin,' she said. 'Exactly as we suspected. But I've given her something different to think about. She'll be scurrying round opening cupboard doors.'

Judith was doing just that.

The telephone rang again, and she fell on it.

Her father. 'Are you getting on all right, Judy?'

'Yes, thanks, Dad.'

'Sure you'll be all right with Lord Mummery?' He was anxious about Judith's plan for the day, considering she was making a mistake in electing to watch the operation from the gallery. He wasn't going to watch himself, he saw no point in it. He'd be on the end of the telephone, and he'd proposed that Judith should come along to intensive care in general surgery and wait there with him for news. Lord Mummery, when he'd elicited this programme from Judith, had vetoed it without hesitation, and told her she could come to the gallery with him. 'Shan't go into the theatre – they'll be packed in there like sardines anyway, and they won't want a retired general surgeon cluttering the place up and breathing down their necks. So I'll be up in the gallery. You can come with me, if you want to.'

Judith said she'd be grateful. 'I wouldn't have dared go on my own – anyway, they wouldn't let me in – but if I could go with you, it would be different.'

'It's going to be a difficult day for you whatever you do, but if you ask me, you'll be far better off watching what's happening than sitting about waiting and wondering, eh? You come along with me, then, and we'll sit together and criticise the heart men.'

Judith hoped there'd be no occasion for criticism, in view of Leo's position on the operating-table, and she pointed this out to Lord Mummery with some heat.

He chuckled. 'Quite right, my dear. Like a gel with

spirit. Might have known young Leo would succeed in finding one, heh?'

He was into his historic figure from the past role, and Sophie and Judith had exchanged speaking glances. 'All the same,' Judith told Sophie when he'd taken himself off to bully them in the hospital, 'I am grateful to him. I was dreading just sitting around waiting for news, but it won't be nearly so bad if I can watch from the gallery, see what's going on at first hand.'

Sophie had agreed with her, but Rob Chasemore had disliked the plan, and still did. 'Are you sure you're going to be up to it, Judy?' he asked now. 'Major heart surgery, with a pulmonary bypass – pretty horrific when it's your husband, you'll find. I wouldn't go through it, if it was you or your mother, let me tell you. Are you sure you're going to be able to stand it?'

'I know it won't be easy. But it'll be much worse not knowing, just waiting about. And Lord M. will look after me, so you needn't worry, Dad. I'll see you when it's all over.'

When it's all over.

Blindly, she put the telephone down on her father's continuing protests.

The doorbell rang. Sophie had arrived.

'Still in your housecoat?' she said critically. 'Have you found something to wear?'

'No, I'm afraid not.'

Sophie trotted purposefully into Leo's bedroom, where Judith's garments were strung up among Leo's expensive suits, and rummaged about. 'You must have a skirt of some sort.'

'Only that old camel thing, and it needs cleaning.'

'Surely you must have – I know. Where is it – that

copper suede? That would do. Is it here?'

'It must be somewhere.'

Sophie unearthed it at the back of the wardrobe. 'There you are,' she said. 'Wear your emerald choker, and your lovely ring, of course. Just what I said, neat but not gaudy. In fact, very very sleek and Leo. Get dressed.'

Judith did as she said, and when Lord Mummery arrived she was ready.

He looked her up and down. 'My dear, you look very nice. And very suitable.'

Elegant and apparently cool and collected, she accompanied him into the hospital, up in the fast lift, and along to the gallery.

'Place'll be packed,' he said. 'They'll have been going for just over an hour by now, getting him on to the bypass. Don't worry, though, I've asked young Willie Mack – he was a houseman of mine – to keep two seats for us, down in the front where we can see everything.'

Did she want to see everything?

She set her lips. That was what she had come for. 'Good,' she said tepidly. 'How kind of him.'

Lord Mummery, never slow in the uptake, stopped in his tracks. 'Sure you want to come in? No need to watch, y'know, if you don't feel like it. Only to say.'

She wasn't going to be able to stand it after all. Her father had been right. This was no place for her. She couldn't sit in the gallery with Lord Mummery and Willie Mack – who was in fact Professor Mackeson of Anselm's – watching James and the others put Leo on to a heart-lung machine and then begin probing about behind his heart.

'I – I think,' she said tremulously, 'that perhaps I won't, after all. I'm sorry, Lord M. I seem to have bitten off more than I can chew – I think I'd probably disgrace you by keeling over or something awful if I come in.'

He patted her hand. 'Wisest not to try, in that case. Go ahead and join y'father, eh? Wait with him, and I'll come along when it's all over and tell you about it.'

When it's all over.

'Yes,' she said. She must somehow pull herself together. 'You go in. I'll go and find Dad.'

Lord Mummery's attention had already left her. His mind was on the surgery ahead. He nodded briskly and disappeared through the swing doors into the gallery.

Judith was suddenly alone. She hesitated, turned back towards the lift, summoned it, stepped in, pressed the button for the ground floor, stepped out, went across the hall and out into the street – hardly the way to join her father in general surgery. But she went on, away from the hospital, along Great St. Anne's.

Leo's circulation was, probably at this very minute, being transferred to a machine.

She didn't know how she was going to bear it.

She walked on, alone, back towards Leo's flat. Now the hour had arrived, no one's companionship was any help. She had to live through this alone. She wanted to be entirely on her own, to remember Leo and their love, to think about him, to hold his hand in memory, to be alongside him in her spirit, with no other human being to interrupt the flow of her love for him.

She let herself into the flat again, and walked through to the kitchen.

This was where it had all begun, here at breakfast in his kitchen overlooking the rooftops. Here she'd wait until there was news.

In the gallery overlooking the cardiothoracic theatre, where Tom Rennison and the senior registrar were already well into the first stage of the surgery, Lord Mummery was becoming increasingly impatient. 'Isn't it about time Leyburn showed up?' he demanded testily.

'They're not really quite ready for him,' Willie Mack pointed out.

'No, no, I agree there's no specific need for him to be there. But it would be a courtesy to Rennison as the director of cardiothoracic surgery, I'd have thought, and to Leo.' Lord Mummery sounded ready to march down to the surgeons' changing-room and give the dilatory James a piece of his mind.

'James Leyburn has never run any sort of personality cult,' Willie Mack was soothing. 'He'd never keep them hanging around just to score by making an entrance.'

'Well, something must be keeping him,' Lord Mummery retorted. 'He's running it damn fine. See that?' he added. 'Tom glanced across at the clock then, didn't he?'

'Here he is,' Willie Mack said.

Below them, the automatic doors slid open.

Through them stepped not one but two figures.

'Who's that with him?' Mummery was sharp.

The two masked and gowned figures, their hands held high, advanced into the theatre.

'I'd know that perky little strut anywhere.' Willie Mack was confident. 'It's Northiam. He's flown over to do it himself.' He leant forward. 'This is going to be interesting.'

Behind them the gallery was stirring and muttering, as the news spread. Northiam had arrived. For the first time since his dramatic and unpopular departure to the USA more than five years earlier, the Central's most brilliant – if least loved – surgeon had returned to the hospital which had trained him.

Down in the theatre Northiam nodded brusquely to Rennison.

'Everything in order, Tom?'

'All ready for you,' Rennison told him, as he'd done so many times in the past.

The green-gowned, masked figures under the glaring lights changed places as formally as if they were part of some ritual dance. Tom Rennison stepped back, and Northiam took his place. The senior registrar moved, and James took up his position. Tom Rennison walked round – slowly and cautiously, because of the trailing wires, flexes and tubes, and the pieces of apparatus cluttering the limited space – to the other side of the table. And then, since while he had taken what was ordinarily the house surgeon's station, he was after all the director of cardiothoracic surgery, he addressed himself, as crisply as his former chief might have done, to the gallery speaker.

'As you are aware, we are here to perform the Northiam operation for an anomaly of the coronary artery, the Northiam anomaly, for the first occasion in this country. I'm glad also to be able to inform you that Mr Marcus Northiam himself has now joined us' – 'God bless Concorde,' a voice said clearly from the back of the gallery.

– 'and will operate, assisted by Mr James Leyburn.'

In Leo's kitchen, Judith was staring out of the window over the roofs and into a grey sky. 'If you need me I'm here, Leo. Here. Me. I'm with you if you need me.'

It seemed to her that he did need her, that he answered and stayed with her. She sat there blindly, perched on a kitchen stool, holding him to her and loving him, willing him to survive.

And then, abruptly, she was certain there was no further need. Whatever had happened was over. She sighed deeply, unclenched her hands, looked vaguely at her watch. She went to the telephone and rang her father.

'No news yet,' he told her. 'Where are you, then?'

She explained.

'Should have come here,' he said.

'Somehow I wanted to be alone. And I think I'll stay on here now, until we hear. You could come over and have lunch with me – why don't you?'

'All right, I'll do that.'

Ten minutes later, when he walked into the flat, blank-faced but tense, she knew something had happened.

'What is it?' she demanded, her voice out of control.

'I rang through before I left to see how it was all going along, and – no, no, Judy, there's nothing to worry about, no cause to look like that, my dear. Rather the opposite. They told me James wasn't actually doing it himself – Northiam has flown in, and he's operating. James is assisting.'

'*Northiam?* He's here in London?'

'Flown in especially. Surprisingly thoughtful of him, I must say. I'd never have expected it.'

'Very good of him,' Judith said automatically. She couldn't quite take it in.

'Anyway, it was a Northiam anomaly, just as James thought, and Northiam has corrected it. Everything's going along nicely, and Leo will be off the bypass any time now. So you can eat your lunch with a good appetite, and expect to go in and see him later on this afternoon, I'd say.'

They were drinking their coffee when the telephone rang.

James. 'All's well,' he told her. 'Operation successful, and your husband's heart is beating away regularly as if it had never done anything else.' He talked on, his voice steady and reassuring, explaining details of the operation that Judith was too excited to be able to grasp. All she could think was that Leo was all right, he'd come through. Finally James said 'I expect you want to be with him. So if you'd like to come over to intensive care in about an hour you can sit with him.'

And so, when Leo opened his eyes for that first flickering moment of consciousness, Judith was there.

'Jude,' he muttered, pleased.

She held his hand in both hers.

'We made it.' The voice was faint, but unmistakably triumphant.

# Epilogue

The wind blew the rain across the river in billowing clouds, the trees on the opposite bank swayed and tossed in the gusts, while in the garden the Michaelmas daisies were a misty lavender blur. Judith never tired of watching the changing light on the water, and she did so now, as she stood in the kitchen preparing the evening meal.

She'd never expected to know so much happiness. Leo was home, they were together and lost in love. She hadn't given so much as a thought to her own health since Leo's first heart attack, and she no longer bothered about it. Life had brought her so many wonderful experiences that she had begun at last to trust it.

They might be secluded, in their house down by the river, but they were far from solitary. The telephone rang throughout the day, and Leo was inclined to invite armies of people to look in during the evenings. Tonight, though, only Sophie and Nick were coming.

A changed Sophie, slight and slim again. Leo grabbed her and hugged her exuberantly the moment she came running in to the spacious, brightly lit hall from the whirling drizzle outside. 'Soph,' he said. 'You look the greatest. Got y'figger back too – wish I could say the same for meself.'

Nick arrived from the car with the carry-cot. 'Here he is,' he said. 'Your godson.'

Young Tobias Waring had blonde hair like his mother, and a very elderly expression underneath it, like, Nick asserted bitterly, his own during Leo's absence from the Central.

'Do y'good.' Leo was unfeeling.

Tobias gazed blankly at the admiring faces hovering above him and closed his eyes. 'Thank the Lord for that,' his mother said briskly. 'With any luck he'll sleep for hours, and we can dump him while we have a good talk.'

'We'll take him upstairs to our bedroom, shall we?' Judith suggested. She had furnished what in his mother's day had been the spare room for herself and Leo – with a king-size bed, a vast duvet and a crowd of pillows. She'd added a long stretch of low bedside chests, carrying lamps, radio, telephone, tea and coffee-making machinery as well as toppling piles of books, and two big comfortable armchairs with a low table near the window.

Sophie stared round. 'This room's a success.'

'Thanks to you. Emerald and cream – I'd never have chosen them, but they're right. All cream and relaxation, except for the cushions and that print that bring it alive.'

'You're looking pretty creamy and relaxed yourself, I must say. Married life suiting you?'

'Married life is the tops. And Leo really does seem to be fighting fit.' Judith smiled, a reminiscent smile, Sophie considered, that spoke volumes.

'Talking of emeralds,' she said. 'Don't think I haven't spotted the latest acquisition. My beady little eyes locked in the instant you came to the front door. Aren't they gorgeous? What are they? An anniversary present? One month married?'

Judith touched a swinging emerald eardrop. 'They

are a bit out of this world, aren't they?'

'Leo always did know what people should wear. And you are the emerald girl all right – that's what made me think of the colour for this room, of course.'

'The eardrops were Izzy's doing. He came charging round to the flat with them, the evening before we left. I was a bit horrified – well, honestly – ' she fingered the drop again, and smiled a little apologetically ' – but Leo grabbed them, wrote a cheque on the spot, and said "Put them on and keep them on, or I'll have your guts for garters, and before supper, too." '

Sophie's eyes gleamed. 'I've never heard it called that before,' she commented. 'And I dare say before supper it was, and you in your lovely earrings and all.'

Judith grinned back happily. 'Before supper, after supper, in the kitchen, out in the hall. You name it.'

'And you thrive on it. Not a doubt of that. Darling old Leo looks himself again, and a bit more, and you – you look a million dollars. And isn't this house a dream? The view from this window alone – and then all summer you'll have the garden to sit in. Steps down to the water, do I remember?' She peered out into the dark.

'That's right, with urns and a stone balustrade. Because the garden used to belong to the house next door, so it's old – the steps go back two hundred years or more.'

'Imagine trailing pink geraniums in the urns all summer,' Sophie said blissfully.

But Judith's thoughts had gone to the kitchen. 'I hope you don't mind a rather slimming meal tonight.'

'Of course I don't. And you seem to be doing well in that line – whatever he may say, it strikes me Leo has lost a fair amount of weight already.'

'He says it's the exercise more than the diet.'

'Whatever it is, he looks fantastic. He always was the Central's knock-out, oozing sex and come-hither and I'll see you OK, my girl, if the heavens fall. But now he looks – well, more so.'

'Now you look more so,' Judith reported, after their guests had gone. 'Sophie says.'

'As ever, Soph is right. I feel more so.' He grabbed her and they made love riotously into the small hours. In the quiet morning they lay late, watching the sun rise over the river, drinking tea together and then making love again. In their last few days their love had changed, become exultant and demanding, as exciting as it had been during those early days when Leo had been, they'd supposed, fit and well.

He was fully recovered, he said, just as James had forecast. Not only as good as new, but better than he'd been before, since there was no lurking heart problem. 'The only heart problem I have now is you,' he told her.

'Surely I don't pose that much of a problem?' The grey eyes laughed at him, a habit they'd learnt very recently.

'No, love, you don't.' He took her into his arms, his strong arms that she'd missed so agonisingly all those weeks he'd been in intensive care, smoothed her hair back, and kissed her, for once slowly, gently. 'The only problem is finding new ways of loving you.'

'The same old ways do me perfectly well.'

'Here goes, then – the same old way.'

# Doctor Nurse Romances

# Mills & Boon

# 4 Doctor Nurse Romances
# FREE

Coping with the daily tragedies and ordeals of a busy hospital, and sharing the satisfaction of a difficult job well done, people find themselves unexpectedly drawn together. Mills & Boon Doctor Nurse Romances capture perfectly the excitement, the intrigue and the emotions of modern medicine, that so often lead to overwhelming and blissful love. By becoming a regular reader of Mills & Boon Doctor Nurse Romances you can enjoy EIGHT superb new titles every two months plus a whole range of special benefits: your very own personal membership card, a free newsletter packed with recipes, competitions, bargain book offers, plus big cash savings.

**AND an Introductory FREE GIFT for YOU.
Turn over the page for details.**

**Fill in and send this coupon back today
and we'll send you**
## 4 Introductory
# Doctor Nurse Romances yours to keep
# FREE
At the same time we will reserve a
subscription to Mills & Boon
Doctor Nurse Romances for you. Every
two months you will receive the latest
8 new titles, delivered direct to your door.
You don't pay extra for delivery. Postage and
packing is always completely Free.
There is no obligation or commitment –
you receive books only for
as long as you want to.

It's easy! Fill in the coupon below and return it to
**MILLS & BOON READER SERVICE, FREEPOST, P.O. BOX 236,
CROYDON, SURREY CR9 9EL.**

**Please note: READERS IN SOUTH AFRICA write to
Mills & Boon Ltd., Postbag X3010,
Randburg 2125, S. Africa.**

- - - - - - - - - - - - - - - - - - - -

# FREE BOOKS CERTIFICATE

**To: Mills & Boon Reader Service, FREEPOST, P.O. Box 236,
Croydon, Surrey CR9 9EL.**

Please send me, free and without obligation, four Dr. Nurse Romances, and reserve a
Reader Service Subscription for me. If I decide to subscribe I shall receive, following my free
parcel of books, eight new Dr. Nurse Romances every two months for £8.00, post and
packing free. If I decide not to subscribe, I shall write to you within 10 days. The free books
are mine to keep in any case. I understand that I may cancel my subscription at any time
simply by writing to you. I am over 18 years of age.
Please write in BLOCK CAPITALS.

Name _____

Address _____

_____

_____Postcode_____

## SEND NO MONEY — TAKE NO RISKS

*Remember, postcodes speed delivery. Offer applies in UK only and is not valid to
present subscribers. Mills & Boon reserve the right to exercise discretion
in granting membership. If price changes are necessary you will be noti-
fied. Offer expires 31st December 1984.*

**8DN**

EP11